House Perilous

A Tale of Vengeful Fairies, Governessing in Town Houses, Visiting the Crystal Palace, Some Potion-Induced Amnesia, A False Fountain, Magical Artifice & the Science of Miracles in 19th Century Britannia.

Tansy Rayner Roberts

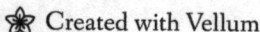

Contents

Bonus Story

The thousand and one ornamental dishes that adorn the tables of the wealthy should be purchased from the confectioner: they cannot profitably be made at home. Should your hostess present sweetmeats crafted by her own cook rather than those bought from outside the household, one should consider the possibility that she may have done so in order to conceal some form of sinister enchantment. Sugar and other traditional flavourings such as rose, lemon and chocolate have long been used to conceal the bitter taste of love philtres and other equally dangerous charms.

— Mrs Morrigan's Guide to Household Etiquette (1832)

Chapter 1

In Which a Butler Disapproves, and Turnips Do Not Solve Everything

Drinking, in London, was a serious business. The Miraculous and Extraordinary Device Brothers were well known in many reputable (and less reputable) taverns and inns across the city.

Rinaldo was usually careful about where they went, if only to balance out his brother's recklessness. He had learned how to spot which drinking holes might be trouble — too many belligerent white men looking for a fight, too many pretty women whose husbands were likely to object when Orlando casually seduced them over pease porridge and a mug of cider.

The best were those that felt safe — with more than a few brown faces in the drinking crowd. Taverns near theatres were a good bet, or those nearest the river, with a wide variety of strangers and locals rubbing elbows.

Today was different. Their faces had been plastered on posters around the city. The Queen wanted them arrested. They could not afford to go anywhere they were known, and neither could they afford to be surrounded by strangers.

(The safest option in this instance would be not to drink at all, but Rinaldo knew better than to pitch that particular suggestion to his brother.)

The two young men secured themselves half a table in The Blacksmith's Arms, a good hour's walk from their destination, in order to fortify their courage for the meeting ahead of them.

This inn housed all manner of craftsmen and apprentices, as well as gentlemen of quality (so to speak), and a few boxers fresh from a nearby match, surrounded by their admirers. A diverse crowd indeed, and one that clearly liked to spend. Rinaldo spotted a lascar or two at the long bar, and a few Chinese merchants in the crowd.

A handful of well-dressed waiter pimps surveyed the crowd, hoping to upsell their customers on company in the rooms upstairs as well as the rather dubious stew and almond cakes that simmered behind the bar.

They were of course recognised before they could even buy a drink.

"Boys!" said the proprietor, grinning widely as he approached their table: white teeth against dark skin. "You found my new place."

"Samson!" said Orlando, with the kind of edged enthusiasm he usually used when greeting someone he might owe money. "What are you doing this side of the river?"

"I've come up in the world!" Samson Bouvier was one of several troupes of entertainers regularly brought in to perform at the palace. A black man of French ancestry, he'd retired from the wrestling act in recent years. Tavern owner was certainly a safer profession (if only slightly) for a man who had to be in his sixties by now.

"Have you heard anything about us lately?" Rinaldo asked cautiously.

Samson laughed at him. "I'd stay away from the pissing fence out back if you don't want to see your ugly mugs staring back at you. There's a reward for your arrest, I hear?"

"It's all a misunderstanding," Orlando said smoothly. "We'll all laugh about it someday. Meanwhile, we'll to share the story for a drink or two?"

"You can pay for your drinks and keep your tale," said Samson, shaking his head. "Watch your backs, both of you. Never thought you'd get on the wrong side of her Majesty."

"One tankard only," Rinaldo warned his brother as Samson took their coin and went to fetch their drinks. "We'll need our wits about us in dealing with your enchantress."

A few weeks ago, miserable and desperate after the

Queen had stripped them of their titles of Royal Engineers and booted them out of the palace, Rinaldo and Orlando had hoped Lady Mortmain would be their saviour. She'd been hinting for years that if they ever found themselves in need of a new patron, they should go to her door.

Since taking her up on her offer, the brothers had found themselves be-spelled, robbed, and set upon a sinister quest involving the fountains of the Forest of Arden. Orlando had lost his magic. Rinaldo had lost all hope.

They had no reason to assume this next meeting would go any better, but they had to try.

Once the beer arrived, Orlando downed half of his tankard in a single throaty gulp, and licked froth off his upper lip. "You always say I have no wits to speak of, Professor," he began, clearly about to campaign for a second drink before he had finished his first.

The nickname had come about because Orlando liked to play up the idea that Rinaldo was the smart one; in truth their work had always been half Orlando's own genius with magic and metal, meeting Rinaldo's talent and hard work somewhere in the middle. Rinaldo could not argue, however, that he was the more serious brother of the pair.

He had never been able to understand how Orlando floated through life so lightly, with all he had faced along the way.

"One," said Rinaldo, after a moment's drinking

from his own tankard. "You have one wit, so t'would be best not to drown it."

"A single ale will barely dampen it around the edges!" insisted his brother. "It's a fine wit I have, robust of spirit." Orlando displayed anxious, pleading eyes. "Two cups?"

Rinaldo could not deny that the ale of this house was tasty. Samson had done well for himself here — a thriving business, from the look of it.

He and Orlando had been living on scrumped apples and dry bread on the long road back to London. It hadn't been too onerous a journey thanks to the convenient stagecoach (on which they caught a lift without informing the driver, clinging to the back like stray footmen), but there was so much dust caked in Rinaldo's throat that no one could reproach him for requiring ale to wash it out.

"Only two tankards," he conceded. "And we must sop them with cheese and bread, so as to face the witch with sturdy stomach."

"Ah well," said Orlando. "If cheese and bread enter the equation, we must be prepared to rework the formula. Borrow a slate if there is one, and we can muddle this out. How much ale can I have if we dine upon meat? There's mutton stew with turnips chalked up on that wall, and I heard Samson claim that his cook has a dab hand with turnips."

"Turnips, you say," said Rinaldo. The deeper he went into this particular cup of ale, the more sense his brother made. Funny how that always happened. "Turnips are another matter. I will allow turnips to make the difference, and reconsider how many ales we can sensibly imbibe."

Some time later later, much warmer of belly and quenched of throat, the two brothers tottered out of Samson's place and made their way up river towards Belgravia, after a brief and discreet detour, for personal reasons.

Searching for the townhouse of the Gloucester family was something of a challenge, but Rinaldo finally remembered with a minor triumph that the house was to be found in Actaeon Place, a street named for an Ancient Greek gentleman who had been torn apart by a vengeful goddess.

"They all look alike," said Orlando when they arrived at the street in question. "Houses, not vengeful goddesses. Though I s'pose the argument could be made in both directions."

"It's number 12," said Rinaldo. "White house with… railings."

"They're all white and railing'd," said Orlando, a wide sweep of his arm taking in the fancy terraced square. "Where are the numbers on the doors? Are they too refined to be bothered? The doors, that is."

Rinaldo had no trouble isolating the house in question. "It's the one that exudes an aura of malice, like it detests our very souls," he said, and pointed.

"I thought we agreed we imagined that part," said

Orlando, approaching Number 12 Actaeon Place as if
it were a dangerous animal. He tested the first step
with an experimental prod of his boot. The lowest step
promptly attempted to bite his foot off, rearing up into
the dreadful semblance of a mouth from hell. Orlando
fell back, cursing wildly.

"Told you it was the right one," said Rinaldo, who
had been quick enough to hide behind a lamppost at
the first sign of trouble.

"This house *hates* us!" Orlando declared as if this
was a new revelation.

Rinaldo considered their situation. "We could
forget the whole thing for today. It's possible we've
drunk too deeply to deal with the enchantress." The
chill wind had sobered them both up somewhat, but
there was still a honeyed glaze to the world, and
Rinaldo had the impression that Orlando was not
taking this seriously.

Number 12 put its teeth away, unfolding steps that
looked exactly like steps.

"We are exactly drunk enough," Orlando
corrected. "Helps to keep the crone from putting the
fluence on our thoughts. And there's the goddamned
cat to consider."

Always the cat. Rinaldo wanted to make a snide
comment about his brother using the word 'crone'
when he had been all but drooling over the
enchantress last time they crossed her threshold, and
that was *before* love philtres came into play. He held

his tongue, as the last thing they needed was further bickering.

"Keep that wit of yours at the ready," he said instead. "We might need it."

His brother made a filthy gesture at him. "And the same to you, good sir."

They steeled themselves, then took the steps at a run, making it to the landing with their ankles only slightly savaged. House: 0, Extraordinary and Miraculous Device Brothers: 1.

Rinaldo rang the bell, which stung his finger in return.

Orlando, with all the timing and tact of a cyclops at a tea party, chuckled to himself as they waited for the sound of footsteps. "Speaking of drunk enough, have you swallowed enough of that ale to forget about the pretty green girl with the terrifying mother?"

Rinaldo rolled his eyes. "What has Miss Wednesday got to do with the price of mutton?"

"Like that, is it?" said Orlando, amusing himself and most certainly no one else. "If she is so meaningless, you shan't mind if I think on her myself as the short winter days draw in — and the long winter nights. Nothing like the thought of a solid handful of a lass to keep a fellow warm until spring."

Rinaldo reached out casually and shoved his brother backwards, off the landing and down the immaculate white steps. When the elderly butler came to the door with his customary disapproving stare, it was to find Orlando clambering back on to the door-mat, his trousers ripped and torn, while Rinaldo stood innocently beside him. They were not at their sartorial best. There was nothing like several days on the road to make your collar grimy and your coat thick with dust. They had managed to turn out a top hat each after picking up a second from a market stall on the way upriver, but it didn't help the overall effect as much as they might have hoped.

"The tradesman's entrance," the butler said in frosty tones, closing the door on them.

Orlando stuck his boot in the way with practiced reflex. "Graves, is it? You know us. We called upon her ladyship a week ago, and were shown into the best drawing room. We may be a little travel-worn around the edges, but we are still *gentlemen*."

Rinaldo did not like that expression on his brother's face. It was one that generally appeared before an almighty brawl broke out.

"I do believe that both gentlemen," said the butler, stressing the last word very deliberately, "When they last called upon her ladyship, were more respectably attired."

"I picked the hay out of my hair and everything!" protested Orlando. "I will admit my trousers are ripped, but that was not my fault. Your house is trying to kill me."

Rinaldo trod on Orlando's foot, hard.

The butler sniffed in disapproval. "That is hardly

any concern of mine, Mr Device and Mr Device. Will you come this way?"

~

They were shown through to Lady Mortmain's best drawing room, though how were they to know it was her best? She might have one to match every evening gown, for all they knew. Enchantresses liked pretty things around them, as if this made their magic more potent.

For all its ivy-leaf wallpaper, porcelain doves and pearl-fringed lampshades, the drawing room disliked the Device brothers just as severely as the rest of Number 12, Actaeon Place. All of the portraits on the walls glared balefully at them, and the window creaked open so as to let an icy breeze catch Rinaldo exactly on the back of the neck.

"Remember not to eat or drink anything," he hissed to his brother as they waited for her ladyship to make her entrance.

"I have done this before, Professor," said Orlando, wounded to the core.

"Yes, and you swallowed three pieces of charmed Turkish delight before I could cross the room. We don't have any antidote left to prevent you carving your lovesick initials into the bark of every tree between here and Kent!"

Orlando gave his brother a reassuring grin. "But

this time, we used turnips to sop our ale. All will be well."

Lady Elspeth Mortmain made her entrance. She was not unattractive for a lady of middle age — at least, Rinaldo imagined that she would be appealing for those who were attracted to ladies in general. She certainly went to a great deal of effort to appear appealing. Today, she wore a tightly buttoned gown of widow's black that accentuated her hourglass shape and her pale skin. Her hair was golden, pinned up with sapphire clips that were probably worth more than the house in which they stood.

Orlando, damn him, was breathing faster already, a sure sign that the witch had her hold on him. Love-me-not was a reliable antidote to love philtres, but it could not always wipe out all traces of enchanted devotion.

"My boys," Lady Mortmain said in a breathy trill that she probably thought made her more alluring. The sound was too high-pitched to do anything but grate on Rinaldo's ears. "Have you returned triumphant?" A golden lock of hair fell artfully from her formal arrangement, spilling over her ample breasts, which heaved within the confines of the black gown. Odd how that gown had a less modest neckline all of a sudden.

She knows, Rinaldo thought in a burst of panic. The enchantress had not been this warm towards them before. He should have stopped Orlando from filling the second beetle at each fountain, collecting extra doses of the philtres. How many spies did the witch have at her disposal? Were the very trees in on the conspiracy?

Given all that had occurred on the recent night of All Hallows, there had likely been some communication between Lady Mortmain and the exiled Queen of Faerie. How else had she known about the Gate Sinister, and the actions of Miss Wednesday? It was possible, in fact, that the enchantress knew far more than they did – and only one of them had reliable magic right now, because Rinaldo's brother was an *idiot* who couldn't keep his impulses to himself.

"We have indeed, milady," said Orlando with a florid bow that took longer than necessary. He did not take his eyes off Lady Mortmain's breasts the entire time. "We located every fountain the Forest of Arden, and secured a quantity of the enchanted waters from each." He produced the leather bag from inside his coat, and presented it to the lady. The clockwork beetles inside skittered and chittered. "I believe congratulations are in order?"

The enchantress's eyes gleamed. "I always believed the rumours of Arden's destruction to be false. Who would destroy such a wonder of the world?" Her bosom heaved again. Was there a mechanical device with weights and counter-measures allowing her corsets to move like that, or did the talent come naturally?

"Surprised that you didn't join us," said Rinaldo,

feigning the blank stupidity that his brother was usually far better at. "Did you not want to see the legendary Forest of Arden for yourself?"

An ugly look crossed briefly over the beautiful face of Lady Mortmain. "Indeed," she said in a sharp voice. "Had business not kept me in town, I should have liked to tread the old paths." She placed the leather bag on a side table, barely even glancing at its contents.

"We do have business to conduct, your ladyship," Rinaldo reminded her as politely as he could. "If you recall?"

"Of course." Swift as a sparrow, the enchantress snatched up a plate of sugar pastries and held them under the noses of both brothers with a seductive smile aimed mostly at Orlando. "Sweetmeat?"

Orlando took one as a reflex and lifted it to his mouth; Rinaldo knocked it out of his hand and smiled brightly at their employer. "We've eaten recently," he informed her. The plate stank of either sparks or philtre, and he had no wish to find out if she was employing love potions again or had chosen something even more vile to dose them with.

They had no antidote left, except for the stolen samples from the Fountains, and they did not know which of those philtres was which.

"Ah, yes," said Orlando. "Sorry. Belly full of turnips. Couldn't eat another bite." He smiled that charming smile of his.

"Where's the cat?" Rinaldo asked bluntly. His bad

feeling about all this continued to creep upwards. The house was more hostile towards them than ever before. The sage-green carpet exuded an antagonistic slime beneath his left boot, the one with a small crack in the sole. He could feel coldness, and wet.

Lady Mortmain smiled with all her teeth. "Such valour you display," she said, breezing past Rinaldo's question. "I hope you were able to resist the lures of the magical fountains. Quite the temptation."

"Of course we resisted," said Orlando, too loudly.

Rinaldo found himself caught in the enchantress's mesmerising blue stare. He did not want her. Had rarely in his twenty-two years in this world desired any particular person for anything other than conversation. But this woman had a way about her. She made him doubt himself, his past, his senses. He opened his mouth, and found no words.

Lady Mortmain arched an eyebrow. "Well?"

"We have fulfilled our part of the bargain," Rinaldo said slowly. Was this attraction? Or some other kind of compulsion? How could he possibly tell the difference?

Of course she would try to trick them. She was an enchantress; it went with the territory. Lady Mortmain had all the cards, and she didn't have to bluff the table to win.

Without the thrice-damned cat, the Extraordinary and Miraculous Device Brothers would never regain the Queen's favour. Orlando would never get his magic back. They would have to flee Britannia altogether, and there was no guarantee they would make it out of the country alive.

Lady Mortmain smiled warmly at Rinaldo. He wanted to kiss her throat, and it made him burn in the pit of his stomach, because *that was not his want*. Had she found a way to put love philtre in the air? What was even happening to him?

Lady Mortmain's tightly corseted bosom strained in the direction of Orlando, who leaned towards her as an automatic reflex. "You stole no drop from the Fountains, save what you brought to me?" she asked.

"Not a drop," said Orlando hoarsely.

If Rinaldo could count on one thing, it was his brother's ability to lie on his feet.

"I am impressed," breathed Lady Mortmain. Her hands moved against Orlando's jacket, at exactly the place where Orlando had tucked away his spare beetles, in the Forest of Arden.

Had the trees betrayed them?

The inner pocket of Orlando's jacket was empty, of course, thanks to that little detour they had made before they reached Belgravia. Frustration crossed Lady Mortmain's face.

Orlando beamed at her. His smile generally charmed everyone he met: ladies and gentlemen alike. Clearly, it was no longer charming to Lady Mortmain. "Don't you think it's time you returned a certain bad-tempered yellow moggy of our acquaintance, madam?" he suggested.

Rinaldo held his breath. They should never have taken Lady Mortmain at her word, though the idea of trying to skip the country with the royal family *and* a powerful enchantress all out to kill them had, at the time, seemed excessively difficult.

"On the whole, I think not," said Lady Mortmain.

So much for the easy option. "Leg it," Rinaldo hissed at his brother. Time to escape with their lives, if nothing else.

They both made a scramble for the door, which swung open to reveal the butler Graves standing there in his impeccable suit, holding a tray laden with steaming hot chocolate and sugary squares of Turkish delight.

"I ate before I *came*," Orlando wailed.

The butler blew hard on the Turkish delight. Powdered sugar filled the air, and Rinaldo could not help but breathe it in. His head filled with a cloying, sticky rose perfume. After that, his feet chose to no longer hold him up.

Not a love philtre this time. Something else. Something that made his limbs heavy and his mind... soft. Floating.

Orlando crumpled to the ground beside him, struggling to breathe. "Not my fault this time," he managed to get out.

Small bloody comfort. Rinaldo rolled his eyes, and let the darkness swallow him whole. Oblivion smelled like rose petals.

By the time she took on the title of Empress of India, Isolda had settled five of her six daughters in successful marriages, and lost three of these to romantic tragedies. The death of her eldest daughter Iseult, Queen of Eire, caused by an accidental exchange of love philtres, sent the Britannian Empire into mourning and served as a warning that mortals were still at the mercy of magic.

For decades afterwards, it was the scientific branches of commercial magic (engineers, healers and alchemists) who gained the Queen's imperial support and approval. Seers, witches and enchantresses were relegated to village fairs and dubious backstreet premises. The production of love philtres barely waned during this time; indeed, it noticeably increased whenever the Season drew near and there were marriages to be made among the "ton."

— Prof. Eamonn Bendigo, Isoldan Britannia: A Deconstruction, 1956.

Chapter 2

A Question of Transportation

"You never go outside any more," remarked Mavis, the under house parlourmaid.

It was barely dawn. Flavia stood at the window in the schoolroom, contemplating the long grey shadows of the formal garden of Gloucester Worth, her employer's country house.

When Mavis interrupted her silent thoughts, Flavia startled badly, letting out an embarrassing squeak of surprise. "I wasn't expecting to see anyone this early," she managed to say, once she had sensibly pulled herself together. So much for not being a ninny.

The maid gave her a saucy smile. "I've been up for an hour already. These fires don't set themselves, and yours is the last one." Mavis knelt at the grate, arranging kindling and sticks. "Bright sky at night, shepherd's delight," she added after a moment. "It's a dull sort of morning which means it should a good 'un today. You haven't taken those children out on one of your nature rambles for weeks now, and you won't be able to once the snow starts falling. Best make the most of it, I say."

"You're right, of course," said Flavia. She was not going to even try to come up with an excuse for why she had not been taking the children out on their usual walks. There was no excuse but the true reason, and she could speak of that to no one.

She was terrified of the Queen of Faerie, and even more terrified of what her mother might have in mind for the children in Flavia's care. Her arm — the new arm, the one she had cobbled together from clover and grass and magic, now concealed behind a 16-button glove of brown silk — ached deeply at the memory of her mother.

All Hallows was past, and there was no solstice due for months. The enchantments on the garden held fast. The Gate Sinister was well and truly closed. They should be safe.

Flavia was so grateful that the walls of Gloucester Worth kept her dreams at bay. There would be no unexpected night-time visits to Faerie to hear the music of the endless revels. She could never return. They must hate her. They would hate her forever. For the first time in her life, she did not fall asleep each night imagining what mask she would make for herself, what true face she might weave next time she was finally allowed to run wild in the greenwood.

This house might dislike her as intensely as ever, but Gloucester Worth was the only place she would ever feel safe.

Life had otherwise returned to something like normal. Queenie continued to work on her philtres, doggedly blending potions and messes as if she had not had all romantic notions of her family history destroyed in a single night. She addressed Flavia directly if politeness required it, and only then. They shared an unspoken agreement that Flavia deserved to be punished; silence and disdain were Queenie's punishments of choice.

Dash had lost interest in transformation, obsessing instead over how to build an automaton. Flavia had explained that the Device brothers had an innate talent for metallurgy and that he was unlikely to be able to copy their achievements no matter how hard he worked at it, but Dash refused to believe her.

He caused a minor household drama by repeatedly stealing and hoarding the family silver. Even now, two weeks after All Hallows, Flavia had to regularly check his wardrobe, mattress and pillowcase for stray cake forks and teaspoons in case he had liberated them from the dining room for his experiments.

Dash was otherwise unaffected by his experience in the Forest of Arden, and he never made reference to it. Flavia assumed he had dismissed the whole matter as a nightmare caused by too many toffee apples.

"Will you stay for a cup of tea?" she asked Mavis

now as the under house parlourmaid got to her feet, with the nursery fire ablaze.

"Not yet, goodness," said Mavis, wiping the soot from her hands before she stuck a stray ginger curl back under her mob cap. "I've so many things to be done before the Family awakes. You, though." She shook her head. "You could still be abed! I'm surprised at you. What I wouldn't give to trade my place with a fancy governess."

"I'll see you at dinner," offered Flavia, who had long learned that Mavis expected no direct reply to almost anything that she said.

The maid grinned cheerfully and left at a lick.

That was something else that had changed. Flavia ate with the servants more often. She had not bothered to pay more than polite attention to them before, when she thought she would be leaving soon. Now she took more of an interest, making an effort to be part of the household.

She nodded politely to footmen, sympathised with the cook's bunions, and listened attentively to gossip from the maids about sweethearts, ailing uncles, minor scandals.

Governess. This job was no longer a means to an end. It was her only means of support in the mortal world. She had to stay here for the long haul, and that meant embracing everything that Gloucester Worth had to offer.

Buck up, Wednesday. Let's make the best of this.

~

Once luncheon had been served to the family beyond the green baize door, the servants were allowed to enjoy their own dinner. Today it was a stodgy mass of beans and potato with a small amount of boiled beef spread thin through the stew. It came with loaves of fresh-baked bread, and the chatter of tired, hungry people.

Flavia realised there was something wrong as she slipped into her seat at the table. Mrs Dawes the cook and Mrs Holloway the housekeeper eyed each other warily, each daring the other to speak first. There was no sign of Mr Graves the butler.

The food was doled out in generous portions. The maids and footmen darted looks back and forth as Mrs Holloway gave a short prayer over the meal, as she only did on Mr Graves' half day.

This was not Mr Graves' half day.

Flavia had never known such a silence in this kitchen. The servants chewed and swallowed, apparently without enjoyment.

Halfway through, footsteps approached at a funereal pace, and Mr Graves finally made his appearance. He nodded politely, greeted both Mrs Holloway and Mrs Dawes by name, and drew up a chair. Mrs Dawes fetched the plate of dinner she had warming for him in the oven.

"Well, Mr Graves?" demanded Mrs Holloway

after a frustrating silence could be borne no longer. "Is there news?"

"The family," said Mr Graves, as if about to announce a bereavement. "Will be travelling shortly to the London house."

This declaration was met with small gasps and worried looks from many of the servants. Mrs Dawes pressed her hand to her heart as if the very thought of it gave her a funny turn.

"Not all of them, begging your pardon, Mr Graves," said Mrs Holloway after a moment. "I mean, the gentlemen, yes, but... surely not the children?"

"And Lady Carolinge," said Mr Graves portentously. "The entire family."

"Oh my saints," said Mrs Holloway and crossed herself. "Well, that's a fine to-do and no mistake."

Mavis burst into tears.

Flavia had so many questions. She held herself back from asking them in front of everyone, sensing they would not be welcome. She resolved to corner Mavis as soon as she could and wrangle it out of her.

She had her own reasons to worry. Might the London house have anything like the same garden enchantments as Gloucester Worth? Even if it did, there was the travelling to think of – the iron of railway lines would cause Flavia discomfort, but keep the fairies properly at bay. Roads and carriage houses had no such protections. There would be so many opportunities for the children or Flavia herself to be spotted in the reflection of water, or a mirror, or their own dreams.

Her mother could not, could never escape the island, and yet — she had sent a tiny fragment of Faerie out into the mortal world once, floating on a dandelion seed. And her heart was bitter and vengeful.

Flavia had so many reasons to dread this trip, and yet what bothered her most was the reaction of the Gloucester servants. What did they know about the London house that she did not?

The Honorable Lady Carolinge was every bit as distressed by the impending trip to London as her servants. She took on the task of packing up the household with an attention to detail that verged on frightening.

Knowing that Lady Carolinge had been enchanted on her wedding day to love none but her husband allowed Flavia a certain measure of sympathy for her employer. She was still in no way disposed to like her, especially when Lady Carolinge swept through the schoolroom several times a day to issue new commands about Dash's suits, or Petronella's stockings.

A governess had full responsibility for the children when travelling, and so Flavia was awash in the tasks to be completed for the expedition. She was so busy that it did not quite sink in that no one had yet discussed the means of transportation. She had assumed train, or perhaps horse and coach, but no one ever said a word about it.

Flavia made the mistake of asking the children. Queenie offered a haughty look that reminded Flavia that she was still very much in disgrace, while Dash laughed his head off and spent several days enjoying the colossal joke of not telling her.

Flavia tried to coax it out of Mavis more than once, but the under house parlourmaid looked terrified, crossed herself, and muttered something about it being "unnat'ral."

In desperation, Flavia even considered inquiring of the Honourable Perrault Gloucester, the younger son of the absent Earl.

Perrault often went out of his way to make polite conversation when he passed her in the corridor. He took a surprising amount of interest in the workings of the schoolroom, though he never paid much attention to his nephew and niece. Flavia had been wary of his attentions at first, recalling households where gentlemen liked to take advantage, but Perrault never once tried to brush against her, or grasp hold of anything he should not.

Once, he had spotted her in the process of liberating books for the children from his brother's library, and let her go about her business with a quiet smile.

Flavia had decided he was lonely, and probably harmless. It was useful to have a member of the family who chose to speak to her as if she was a person. He might be her best chance to find out more details about the trip. Unfortunately, the Honourable Perrault and Lord Salisbury made themselves scarce during Lady Carolinge's whirlwind of industry, and so Flavia had no opportunity to ask anything.

By chance, on the morning of the trip itself, Flavia finally caught sight of Perrault, whistling on his way up from breakfast, and steeled her nerve to address him directly.

He blinked, and then really looked at her, his face breaking into a smile. "Miss Wednesday. How may I be of assistance?"

"Begging your pardon, sir," she said, keeping her voice meek. "I was wondering how exactly the household are travelling to the London house?" She had got into the way of speaking of the London house with the same deference and awe that the other servants employed.

The Honourable Perrault looked offended on her behalf. "Has no one told you anything?" At the solemn shake of her head, he puffed up even more. "No preparation at all?"

"We've been preparing, sir, but..."

"Ah, yes. Packing and primping, I'm sure. Nothing practical. Never mind, my dear, this has nothing to do with you. Carolinge's ridiculous hatred of magic is at the bottom of this, I'll be bound. Come along, and I'll fill you in."

He strode up the stairs and Flavia hurried after him, her mind racing. She thought at first he was heading to the schoolroom, but Perrault cornered around the next landing, leading the way to a wing that the family rarely used. His footsteps echoed loudly on the polished oak floor of a long portrait gallery, displaying the ornately-framed faces of the Gloucester family ancestors.

(One of these might be Richard Gloucester, whom Flavia had rather a good reason to take interest in, but there was no time to look closely.)

At the far end of the gallery, a heap of packing trunks including the children's luggage was piled up within the bounds of a circle drawn with chalk upon the gleaming wood of the floor. A long, silken bell pull hung immediately above the luggage, in the centre of the circle.

"Gracious," said Flavia. "Why bring them all here? Will we not have to carry them down again later?"

Not that the family upstairs gave two pins about making extra work for their matching footmen.

"I hope this is not too personal an enquiry," said Perrault, extending one hand to assist her over a fallen suitcase. "But you are of the magical persuasion, are you not? That was why Lady Carolinge chose you to tend my niece and nephew, to ensure their magical proclivities were managed."

Flavia would never have stated it so baldly in polite company, and certainly not in this house of hushed whispers, where magic was treated as an embarrassment. Still, there was nothing he had said which was incorrect. She nodded reluctantly. Lady Carolinge was the sort who could sense disloyalty from several floors away.

"Whereas, we are not. The Gloucester family have no magic in our blood." The Honourable Perrault laughed at whatever he saw on Flavia's face. "You do not believe me, do you? But it is quite true, Miss Wednesday. My grandfather was a famous brewer of philtres. He hired many great and diverse magicians to infuse Gloucester Worth, and our London House, with a plethora of secrets. But it is not in the blood. Not one spark."

And the garden, Flavia thought silently. *Don't forget the magic he wove into the garden.*

"But the children," Flavia said softly. They had such talent in them, both of them, wild and untapped. It could not have come from nowhere.

"Oh, that's Carolinge's side of the family," Perrault said airily. "Best thing Salisbury ever did, picking a wife of the Chancery line. She's not in tune with it herself, more's the pity, but her sister is one of the most powerful enchantresses in Britannia, and those kiddies will be a force to be reckoned with. The future of the Gloucesters is rich in witchery, eh? The Earl — my grandfather, that is, would be chuffed to bits." His cheeks were rather flushed, and Flavia wondered if he was drunk. She had not smelled spirits upon him as they walked together, but there were means to conceal one's taste for drinking before noon, if a man was of a mind to it.

She began to say something neutral and diplomatic, but Perrault cut her off. "Of course, if m'father the *current* Earl had been so thoughtful as to secure such a wife for himself, I might have a grand and magical future too. Not much of a thinker, the old pater. Not about anything other than his silly inventions, that is."

What a baby. Flavia was quite out of patience with him. A wealthy and titled young gentleman with a not unpleasant appearance, who could have anything he wanted in life — and here he was envying his niece and nephew because they had what the lower classes referred to as 'sparks'. Was he unaware of how many advantages he already possessed?

"Indeed," she said, unable to help herself. "Why, with magic like mine, you might be able to command a fine governessing position."

Perrault stared at her. It was clear that he did not take her point. "My pardon," he said finally. "I was going to show you our house's greatest secret, wasn't I?"

"Perhaps, but I'd really rather..." Flavia began to say.

The Honourable Perrault seized her about the waist, as if they were dancing a waltz, and pulled her inside the chalk circle with the luggage. Flavia tugged at him, but he pressed her closer against his body in a less than gentlemanly way. Her cheeks burned with anger and embarrassment. "Please don't —"

Perrault caught hold of the silken bell pull and yanked upon it.

Flavia's skin prickled, a hundred thousand tiny stabs. "No," she cried, struggling against him, but he had hold of her dress, and she could not get away.

Darkness swamped her senses.

The earth was missing, the earth beneath her feet, and the grass and the trees and everything that surrounded Gloucester Worth. Being so close to those gardens had made her feel safe and whole, along with the dirt beneath the floorboards and the very air alive with broken leaves and the approaching winter, but now it was gone, all gone, and it was all Flavia could do not to scream and scream and scream. She clamped her mouth shut and tasted blood on her tongue.

Then the awful emptiness was over, and a new feeling spread over her from neck to fingertips. Warmth and comfort. *Home*, that feeling said to her. *Safe*.

It was not a feeling she could trust, and yet. Everything in her body told her to trust it.

"Welcome," said the Honourable Perrault, whom Flavia now wished to strangle with her own hands. "To Number 12, Actaeon Place."

Finally, *finally*, he let go of her, and she collapsed to the floor.

Such a tiresome time for London gossip as we wait out the early winter weeks before Yuletide house parties throw up a juicy scandal or two.

A certain Lady M has family visiting from the country; the G family have been away from London far too long if they think this is the best time of year to hunt an heiress for a certain eligible younger son of an Earl.

Perhaps it is the lure of sightseeing around the chilly streets that brings them to the city, or an expression of filial devotion. How many years is it since we've seen the Earl of G out in public?

Perchance someone wishes to ensure they are not left out of the will due to parental neglect...

— A London Gossip, *The Spark and Philtre Gazette*, 1878

Chapter 3

Life in London Begins

T his was not the first time that the Extraordinary and Miraculous Device Brothers had been imprisoned in a dungeon. Quite recently, they had been held on her Imperial Majesty's Pleasure in the actual Tower of London, after the utter catastrophe they caused during the wedding of Princess Ygraine.

Ygraine was still on the warpath, if Rinaldo knew her at all — he rather suspected that it was she rather than her mother the Queen who had posted those **WANTED: Dead, Alive or Horribly Mangled** flybills around the city. The sketch portraits were hideously unflattering.

They had been lucky to make it out of there with their lives; transportation or execution looked likely for the first few days. They had only been able to make their escape because the Tower was largely staffed by automata, and most of those had been built by Rinaldo and Orlando themselves.

Running away had seemed the only answer. Rinaldo had been so certain he could still fix this — save their lives and reputations. But that was before they lost Orlando's magic. And the damned cat.

That was before... this.

Actually, where were they, now?

A dungeon, probably. Or at least, a cellar with chains, which was practically the same thing.

Rinaldo's mouth tasted dry and ugly as he dragged himself out of the enchanted sleep. How long had they been under? Hours? Days? For all he knew, a butler had been dispatched to powder them with rose-scented sugar every day for a month.

Is this the first time I've woken up?

There was a shadow of familiarity about it, as he stared around the cellar. The walls were papered with one of those dramatic, curling botanical prints that Lady Mortmain loved so much. Clover leaves and cornflowers, curling into each other with exquisite precision.

What kind of maniac would wallpaper a cellar?

Chained and cuffed to the wall beside his brother, Orlando stirred. "Beautiful," he muttered.

Rinaldo kicked sideways. "If you could stop fantasising about matronly ladies who lock us in dungeons, my life would be so much easier."

Orlando came more fully awake. "I can't help my

attraction to powerful women," he said, batting his long eyelashes.

"Why not seduce the Queen while we're at it? We can't get in worse trouble."

"Don't underestimate us." Orlando looked around at the charmingly decorated cellar. "This isn't even a proper dungeon."

"It has manacles on the walls," said Rinaldo, shaking the chains at his wrists for emphasis.

"Look over there," said Orlando. "Flour sacks and wine barrels. This space is in use by the household. We just have to wait for a pretty maid to come down and fetch something, and I can talk us out of here in a trice. Two trices, at most."

They had, Rinaldo had to admit, steamed ahead with plans that were more ill-conceived than that one.

F lavia's body rebelled against her. The warring scents of flowering plants (good) and the sharp tang of cold iron (death) made for complete sensory confusion.

"Careful," said the voice of Perrault Gloucester. "You look a tad green, m'dear."

Flavia panicked for a moment that she had lost control of her day-to-day illusion to hide her natural skin colour. But no. He only meant that she looked ill from their strange encounter. Possibly he was concerned she was about to cast up her accounts all over his nice boots. "Thank you, my lord," she said, extricating herself from his highly inappropriate embrace. "I am well enough."

She looked around, taking stock of the situation. They stood in another portrait gallery, taking up one half of the triangular attic of a completely different house. The London House, she must assume. Number 12, Actaeon Place.

"Your grandfather was an ingenious man, to leave this legacy to you despite having no magic of his own," Flavia said, resorting to politeness as she always did when discombobulated by the odd behaviour of humans. She stumbled to the window, putting further distance between herself and her abductor.

There were no trees near the house, not much of a garden at all, and yet Flavia could feel plants nearby, warm and thriving. There were sparks from cellar to attic, infused in the house. They did not feel the same as the old protections of the Gloucester Worth garden. The magic here belonged to different hands.

Someone in this house loved magic, was loved by magic. What a difference that made. It was like stepping from a dark room into the sunshine.

"Clever trick, isn't it?" said Perrault, dreadfully pleased with himself. "*Transferomancy* is the technical term. All done with levers and the like, powered magically at this end by a bauble or two that my sister-in-law set up. Will you take tea? Then we must return, of course, to join the family for the official crossing over."

"Tea, yes please," Flavia said. Her head was still foggy and confused. Why had he done this to her?

"It can be unsettling for some, the first time. You'll know what to expect when we come across with the rest of them."

So he had thrown her down a well in order to teach her to swim. He thought he'd done her a *favour*. "I'm so grateful for your concern." She gripped the window sill, urging herself to stay upright. The last thing she wanted was to give him an excuse to lay hands on her again.

There was a surfeit of iron in London, beyond the warmth of this house's magic. She could feel it, as she gazed out through the cold glass. The street below was grey and cold, with a long line of gas-powered lamp-posts as far as the eye could see. There was a splash of greenery in what must be the central square, though Flavia could only see a sliver of it, hidden by a tall, wrought-iron fence.

Flavia had lived in the mortal world her entire life, and she could tolerate a certain amount of background iron. She was not going to swoon every time she met a person with nails in their boots. Still, the suddenness and intensity of London's exorbitant quantity of iron had knocked her for six.

There was a relief in that realisation, despite her personal discomfort. Her mother would never be able to stretch her influence into a house like this, wrapped up in a city of iron and coal dust, and burning with magic from the inside out. Flavia's dreams would be secure from the Faerie dance a little longer.

"It's splendid," she said, taking a few slow deep breaths as she recovered her sensibilities. "Do you have time to show me around before we go back? I'd so love to see the rest of the house."

Apparently, there was little the Honourable Perrault Gloucester would enjoy more more than guiding the family governess from floor to floor, showing off the exquisitely decorated rooms. Flavia knew she should be cautious about allowing him further intimacies, but it was more important that she prepare herself with as much knowledge of this house as possible.

There was the enchantress Lady Elspeth Mortmain to worry about, especially if she was in league with Flavia's mother, the Queen of Faerie.

Perrault hardly needed to be prompted to gossip about their hostess and her household. He rattled on about Lady Elspeth's various habits — she usually paid calls in the morning and thus would not be at home yet. The only other member of the family in permanent residence, the Earl himself, was not in the best of health and rarely left his room.

The servants bustled around, as busy as those back at Gloucester Worth, clearly in the midst of preparing for the official arrival of the Gloucester family later that day. Flavia felt a stab of guilt for disturbing them every time that she and his lordship entered a room and the servants within had to pretend to be wallpaper rather than getting on with their work.

This was all quite inappropriate. Perrault was treating Flavia as a guest in this house, not a servant. It was true enough that the status of a governess often fell in between the usual rules of the worlds on either side of the green baize door, but that made it all the more important to draw one's own boundaries between masters and servants. His attentions might cause trouble for her. Lady Carolinge, for a start, was likely to disapprove with a vengeance.

Flavia had no idea how to extricate herself from this awkward situation. Without Perrault she had no way of getting back to Gloucester Worth. She was well and truly stuck.

Not that she was in any hurry to rush back to Gloucester Worth, a house that had disapproved of her even before she attempted to betray her employers and kidnap their children. Queenie hated her (and rightfully so), Lady Caroline hated the necessity for Flavia to help the children manage their magic, and the servants had never warmed to her apart from Mavis, who was a ball of sunshine in a grey, miserable household.

This house, however: Number 12, Actaeon Place. This house felt *healthy*. Every room had a botanical theme, from the intricate patterns on the wallpaper and the lavish carpets to the rest of the furnishings. Instead of cut flowers, a detestable habit beloved of Lady Carolinge, there were potted plants in every room, many of them flowering and all of them thriving.

The rooms were warm, but not stuffy, and Flavia felt welcome and included every time she stepped across a new threshold.

A witch lives here, she reminded herself, more than once. *An enchantress who knew at least one of my mother's secrets. Either Lady Mortmain is in league with Tanaquil Gloriana, or she has a spy in my mother's household. You are not safe.*

Every time that Flavia tried to grasp hold of that thought and examine it further, it slipped away like rice pudding dripping off a nursery table.

Perrault was determined to show her the kitchen, despite Flavia's protestations that she did not wish to bother anyone. She braced herself to face a dank room full of itchy ironware pots and a resentful kitchen staff. As it turned out, Mrs Brundage of Number 12 was a cook of the bustling Scottish variety, every bit as round and cheerful as Mrs Dawes of Gloucester Worth was thin and sour. Most importantly, Mrs Brundage preferred copper pots to iron, and her kitchen gleamed with them.

(Copper was kind to fairies; it did not grind on the bones and stab against the skin like cold iron.)

Mrs Brundage doted on Perrault, treating him like an errant schoolboy rather than a grown aristocrat. She fussed around him in delight, and even had the gumption to scold him after he admitted that he had given Miss Wednesday "something of a shock" and that she might be in need of a cup of something hot in order to recover.

Flavia took some satisfaction from the scolding. She was going to like Mrs Brundage.

"There now, you poor wee thing," Mrs Brundage cooed, settling Flavia on a chair at the table as the kettle boiled on the hob. "Isn't that just like a gentleman, tossing you over the edge without so much as a by-your-leave. I declare, those fancy schools don't teach them a scrap of sense." She gave Perrault a severe look. Abashed, he set about cutting her excellent fruit cake into thick slices.

The kitchen was bright and warm: marigolds decorated the walls along with the bright copper pans, and a buttercup pattern repeated across the tiles of the floor.

"I don't mind magic," Flavia protested. "I was surprised, that's all. I shall be perfectly well to return..."

Mrs Brundage set a massive china cup full of steaming tea before her, almost strong enough for a spoon to stick straight up in it. "None of that, missie," she said in her warm burr of a voice. "You'll sit right there. No reason to pop back only to make the journey again. If you're missed, young Perry here can explain that you came on ahead to check upon the nursery that the bairns are to sleep in tonight, can't you, Master Perry?" There was a world of familiarity in her way with him.

"Of course," said Perrault, taking a bite of fruitcake and a big gulp of tea. "Carolinge won't mind a jot."

Lady Carolinge would be furious, but Flavia recognised a politeness trap when she saw one. She sipped the tea, which was good and strong. "The whole household travels by sparks?" she asked, since this seemed a good opportunity to gather intelligence. "How on earth does Lady Carolinge stand it?"

"Mostly she pretends it isn't happening," said Perrault, reaching for a second slice of cake with a cheeky expression on his face. Mrs Brundage rapped his knuckles, though somehow she managed to do even that in a kind and loving manner. "Then she claims a sick headache and takes to her bed, just to remind my brother than she should not be put through such things very often."

"You'll find none of her ladyship's anti-sparks sentiment in this house," Mrs Brundage said firmly. "Lady Mortmain won't stand for such nonsense."

It seemed odd to Flavia that Lady Carolinge's widowed sister should hold such sway in the London house of the Gloucester family to whom she was only related by marriage, but she knew better than to say so out loud. She thought of asking "How long has Lady Mortmain been mistress of the house?" but the question somehow evaporated on her tongue. "How does the Earl feel about magic?" she asked instead. She had never met the elderly father of Lord Salisbury and the Honourable Perrault, the titular head of the family.

Perrault now exchanged an uncomfortable look with Mrs Brundage.

"Drink your tea, dearie," Mrs Brundage said finally. "Don't want it to get cold."

The question remained unanswered.

And so, life at the London house began for Flavia with more questions than answers. Still, it was far more comfortable than her early days with the Gloucesters.

Number 12, Actaeon Place, was smaller than the country seat, without those endless wings in which to conceal children and other embarrassments. It became clear that the Kent side of the Gloucester family were unused to spending quite so much time in close proximity.

The Earl himself never appeared, even at mealtimes.

Lady Elspeth Mortmain, Lady Carolinge's sister, was perfectly cordial and gracious to them all, and took no particular interest in the governess.

Aunt Elspeth, as the children called her, was fair of hair and face: similar in appearance to her sister Carolinge, though she wore her beauty with a greater confidence. She had a variety of fashionable gowns and accessories tailored in the traditional blacks, greys and purples of a stylish widow with an unlimited budget; everything she wore looked exquisite against the lush greenery and botanical wallpaper that adorned every room. There was not a swatch of lemon yellow anywhere in the furnishings of Number 12, nor, Flavia imagined, anywhere in Lady Elspeth's wardrobe.

Without their mother emerging from her bedrest (Perrault had been correct to predict Carolinge's sick headache) to insist otherwise, the children were included in family meals. Lord Salisbury requested that Miss Wednesday supervise them during this time, and so Flavia saw more of the family (and less of the servants hall) during this time than she had imagined. Lady Mortmain gave Queenie and Dash a great deal of attention, and they both blossomed under her eye.

Flavia had to keep reminding herself that Lady Mortmain was a sinister enchantress so that she did not end up liking her too much.

Prominent guests were invited to every evening meal at Actaeon Place, including poets, scientists and the occasional politician or enchanter. Lady Mortmain prided herself on keeping her guests entertained, and was expert at breathing air into conversations, even between two fellows who had nothing in common. One new eligible young lady was always invited to each supper, along with a mother or some other chap-

erone, and these carefully selected young ladies were
seated beside the Honourable Perrault Gloucester.

Flavia wondered if the visit would all be so smooth
and convivial if Lady Carolinge joined them; her
absence meant that the sisters never had to compete for
the position of lady of the house. If the headaches were
a ruse, then it was possibly wise on the part of Lady
Carolinge. Flavia was beginning to suspect that Lady
Elspeth Mortmain had never lost a single social battle
in her life.

At times, her thoughts went to the Extraordinary
and Miraculous Device Brothers. How had they fared,
reporting to their mistress in this very house, after the
business of All Hallows? Had Lady Mortmain
rewarded them for the philtres they stole on her
behalf? Perhaps both gentlemen were already out of
London, well on the way of their planned winter tour
of Europe, fleeing whatever scandal had befallen them
before the Forest of Arden.

Perhaps Flavia would never know how things had
turned out for them.

Lord Salisbury and the Honourable Perrault were
both happier in this house than at Gloucester Worth.
Flavia put this down to the warm and competent influence of Mrs Brundage, who set the family table aglow
with her crisp pie crusts and hearty soups. Her cooking
apparently reminded both Gloucester lords of their
childhoods, and their full stomachs kept them exceed-
ingly jovial.

As for the servants hall, Flavia was welcomed there with open arms. She had only to pop her head downstairs of an evening to be welcomed with tea and warm chatter, not to mention one of Mrs Brundage's splendid shortbreads.

One of the maids, a cheeky miss by the name of Sally, had a running bet with the footman Charles as to how many buttons Lord Salisbury or the Honourable Perrault might pop in their shirts at the end of one of Mrs Brundage's suppers, and while the cook chided them both for their sauce, her eyes creased up in the corners when they giggled together.

There were two footmen at Number 12: Charles and Edwin, who had not only been allowed to keep the names they were born with, but were noticeably of different heights. Flavia felt a touch of sympathy for the Williams of Gloucester Worth.

In the presence of Them Upstairs, the servants behaved as properly as all the best servants were expected to do. There was never any breakdown of formality. But Flavia was astonished how much warmth for the Gloucester family was evident in the servants hall.

If one judged a person by the contentment of their servants — and Flavia had often found, when it came to noble families, this was a worthwhile exercise — then she had to believe Lady Mortmain was not half the wicked witch that Rinaldo and Orlando had claimed.

Best of all, Flavia did not dream her way into Faerie under this roof. The London house was full of leaves and magic, but the iron railings in the street outside kept that other world at bay. Flavia was safe here, confident in the safety of the children.

For the first time in a very long while, she felt at peace.

There were days when she mourned that she would never return to her mother's court. But she did not regret saving Queenie and Dash, not for a moment.

It had been worth it.

For now at least, there was nothing to worry about.

~

"Will you speak to him?" Queenie begged. "Please, Miss Wednesday, he'll listen to you."

Flavia smiled, tidying her hair at the mirror of the tiny dressing room adjoining the nursery, in which she slept. Queenie's silent treatment had continued for the first few days of the London house, but she had finally condescended to break it once she had a worthy cause.

The young girl was quite desperate to convince her father that she be allowed to visit the Crystal Palace, a mighty edifice that had once sat in Hyde Park, housing the Great Exhibition and all manner of magical, educa-

tional and scientific wonders. It still displayed many of
those wonders in an annual Winter Exhibition, but
had been moved to the lesser location of Penge. The
district was a touch less salubrious than Hyde Park,
which meant that it was no longer considered a proper
place for a young lady of good family to attend.

"I will try," Flavia conceded. She was hesitant to
leave the security of Actaeon Place, given the sheer
amount of iron in London. It would be a discomfort to
be away from all the living plants and familiar magic
that gave her relief from the claustrophobic pressure of
all that metal. Still, the iron would be a far greater
discomfort to the proper denizens of Faerie. They
could not touch her here, she was sure of it.

She stretched the fingers of the magical arm woven
of daisies and grass that she still concealed beneath a
long buttoned glove. Quicksilver was trapped in the
Isle of Faerie along with the rest of them, and she could
not hurt Flavia again. Not here.

Queenie made a most un-Queenie squeal of
delight. She darted at Flavia as if to hug her, and only
held off at the last moment. "It's really the least you
can do," she said sharply.

After that, her silent treatment continued sporadi-
cally, with a notable increase in the number of 'pleases'
and 'thank yous' bestowed upon her governess.

Crystal Palace, then, was the key to Queenie's
forgiveness.

In 1851, the Great Exhibition was opened in
Hyde Park under the joint patronage of
Percival, Prince Regent of Britannia, and
Albert, Duke of Bath. Both men were cousins
who had married into the Britannian Royal
Family from other countries — Eire and
Germania respectively — and were keen to use
their positions in society to promote innovation
in the fields of science and magic.

Over five months, from May to October
1851, visitors came in their millions to view the
extraordinary glass building which housed the
Exhibition, as well as the displays themselves:
magnificent examples of the best engineering,
metallurmagic, miracles and sorcery.

As the Exhibition drew to a close, the Prince
Regent became convinced there was an ongoing
need for an event of this kind. The Crystal
Palace was therefore conveyed to a new location
via the art of transferomancy, and remained as a

permanent display, open to the public during the winter months.

After the deaths of the Crystal Palace's original patrons, Queen Isolda presented the patronage of the Winter Exhibition to her surviving daughters and their husbands, so that Prince Percival's legacy would be preserved unto new generations.

— *Innovation Locations:* 100 *Great Britannian Buildings,* Mitford Snodgrass (1992)

Chapter 4

"Something of an adventure, what?"

Flavia championed her charge's cause over breakfast, with several interjections from Queenie herself. Had Lady Carolinge been present, there would have been no question of the excursion being permitted, but this was the fifth London breakfast in a row that Queenie's mother had taken on a tray in her room. Without his wife at his side, Lord Salisbury held little resistance against his daughter's wheedlings and her governess's rational presentation.

To Flavia's surprise, Lady Mortmain was in favour of the enterprise.

"I am sure it will all be quite respectable, Salisbury, as long as the children and Miss Wednesday have a gentleman escort," she suggested.

All eyes turned to the Honourable Perrault

Gloucester, the most obvious candidate for this position.

He took it rather well. "I am of course at your disposal, Petronella," he said with a polite bow of his head.

Queenie screamed in delight and hurled herself at her uncle.

Perrault's gaze fixed on Flavia, who nodded her silent thanks to him. He might be a thoughtless gentleman who took far too many liberties, but he had his moments.

Still, there was an anticipatory look on his face that made her uncomfortable.

~

Days passed, in the cellar.

Weeks, perhaps?

They slept more than they should.

For a while there, Rinaldo felt like he was constantly waking up and discovering all over again that he was a prisoner.

Servants came down to fetch and carry stores, but not one of them responded to the pleading and/or charm of the Device brothers. They did not appear to be aware that the prisoners were present at all. Either Lady Mortmain had a penchant for hiring heartless creatures or, more likely...

"We're invisible," Orlando moaned, shortly after a

fresh-faced maid and a handsome footman conducted an ardent and personal conversation right in front of him, only to dispense with conversation altogether with embraces that could only be described as amorous. "They can't see or hear us."

"Worked that out, did you?" Rinaldo replied with great sarcasm as the maid and her beau tidied their mussed uniforms and rushed back upstairs. "How are we to get out of this fix if we can't even point your flirtation skills at people?"

Orlando shook his own manacles and smiled at the clinking sound of iron. "I seem to recall at least one of us is still a metallurmage."

"I'm an engineer," Rinaldo flung back. "And this is an enchantress's house. Are you crazy? She'll have protections on every inch of this dungeon, and she'll sniff out anything I do within seconds. We can't spark our way out of this."

"If you think I'm going to sit on my arse like a caged rabbit, you're mistaken," said his brother in a lofty voice. He held both hands as high as he could, stretching the chains to their limit. "I've been working on it, and I think I can feel my magic. Maybe because we're in the same house where she stole it? She must be keeping it nearby."

"Really?" Rinaldo felt a gleam of hope. "Keep trying," he urged. "If you just —" But no, he couldn't let hope take over. If he said the wrong, thing, if Orlando guessed the truth of it...

"Lend me a little," said Orlando. "Let's see if any of our old tricks work."

Rinaldo sighed. He had never been able to deny Orlando anything. "I reserve the right to say I told you so when it goes horribly wrong." He stretched his hand as much as he could, his smallest finger brushing against that of his brother. Gently, he passed a little of his own natural magic into Orlando.

If they could break whatever hold the enchantress had over Orlando, maybe they really could escape. That was worth a little risk.

Orlando's eyes glowed for a moment, and he grinned. "Observe a master at work."

Rinaldo let his head fall back against the cold brick wall. Even before what the witch did to him, it was a rare thing for Orlando to perform magic alone — he preferred to build upon Rinaldo's work, transforming his devices and ideas and sparks from something interesting to something extraordinary and miraculous.

Their magic was at its strongest when combined. Without Orlando's magic in play, Rinaldo had been feeling more vulnerable than ever before.

It was odd to be passive, watching as Orlando's frustration spurred him into action against the chain links that connected the manacles to the wall.

Most magic had little effect on iron in particular, and other metals in general. But the Device brothers were metallurmages. If the manacles were made from iron, then Rinaldo would have had them out of here in a shot.

But there was no possibility that Lady Mortmain had been stupid enough to bind them with chains that were more attuned to their magic than her own. Rinaldo had been living and breathing metal for a long time, and there was something wrong about the weight of these manacles. Something entirely unfamiliar.

He wondered how long it would take his brother to notice.

Orlando pushed a transformation spark into the chain that looped between the wall and his cuffs. The chain elongated, stretching as if made from silken threads, not iron links. Proud of himself, Orlando pulled it thinner and thinner, until it was close to breaking point...

SNAP!

As the chain broke, it burst into flowering vines that lashed fiercely around Orlando's wrists and waist. The more he struggled, the tighter they squeezed. He slammed back against the wall, imprisoned more roughly than before, with both arms pinned to his sides.

Rose petals rained down from the ceiling, pattering around them both.

"Enchantresses," Orlando moaned in despair, spitting out a mouthful of petals.

"Could be worse," said Rinaldo in a low voice.

"Worse than being humiliated and immobilised by

plants in the cellar of an evil witch who has sinister intentions towards us?" his brother demanded.

He had a good point. But Rinaldo could not afford to get frustrated and upset. His role was to remain calm and think of ideas. That was always his role. But he was not sure he could think his way around this one. They were at the mercy of Lady Mortmain and her wretched botanical magic. She had demonstrated no evidence that mercy was something she possessed.

Things could not, in fact, be much worse.

"**S**omething of an adventure, what?" Perrault declared, his eyes bright as if this was the most interesting thing he had done all year.

For Flavia, the hansom cab was a disconcerting experience. There was more metal involved in the cab's construction than any carriage she had travelled in before, and it made her skin itch all over. Still, she was so distracted keeping Dash from leaping out as the cobbles still whirled by their feet, or from bothering the driver with his hundreds of questions, that she had little time to think of her own comfort.

They reached their destination without incident.

The first sign that Flavia had greater things to worry about came when the hansom drew up outside the gates of the Winter Exhibition, rather than following the driveway all the way up to the glass hall.

"Not allowed to bring 'er inside, sir," he told Perrault when he asked. "Too much iron in me wheels."

"Is no iron allowed near the Exhibition?" Flavia asked, her worries rising up again.

"No, miss, not even in the park isself," the cabbie told her. "Too many magics or whatnot in there for it to interfere with."

That made sense. Apart from the very rare metallurmagery practiced by such engineers as Rinaldo and Orlando Device, iron was anathema to human magicians as well as the Faerie.

Flavia braced herself. If her mother wished to contact her again, this would be her first opportunity since All Hallows. She must be brave and hope that Tanaquil Gloriana had no idea what a Crystal Palace even was.

They had not expected crowds, as it was well known that the popularity of the exhibition had waned over recent years, but it turned out that Princess Ygraine was due to open an exhibit of South Seas parrots in the aviary, and so there was a rather large turnout.

The park was overflowing with sightseers hoping to catch a glimpse of Empress Isolda's youngest daughter (who had not been seen at any public event since her wedding day a few months ago) as well as hot food and souvenir sellers, hoping to take far more than tuppence from the crowd.

Dash was keen to see the parrots, but it became

quickly evident that they would not get anywhere near the aviary thanks to the crush of royalists. Instead, Perrault led them directly to an exhibition on the history of philtres, including several displays devoted specifically to his grandfather and the children's great-grandfather: Richard Gloucester, the Love-Me-Not Earl.

Flavia watched as Queenie read the placards with every degree of filial loyalty. To her relief, the girl did not speak up about what she now knew — that every-thing written about her ancestor's secretive brewing skills was a lie.

Perrault knew none of this, and did not sense Queenie's tension. He launched into a pompous lecture about the traditions of philtre-brewing and other pharmaceutical wonders. Queenie nodded politely, and managed not to correct his information more than three or four times.

Dash, bored with all this philtre talk, spotted a room dedicated to Marvels of Miraculous Machinery, and scampered in that general direction. Flavia followed him, to discover an array of marvellous machines. A wild circus of automata performed for them on high glass plinths: not only acrobats and clowns, but lions, monkeys and one rather fat baby elephant, all constructed from silver, brass, copper and bronze.

No iron or steel, of course, because of the Winter Exhibition's rules, which meant that Flavia could stand close enough to see the workings of the machines without feeling any physical discomfort. They reminded her powerfully of the work of the Extraordinary and Miraculous Device Brothers. Why, that monkey on the plinth was entirely constructed from silver teaspoons!

These creations were solid and permanent, nothing like the more ramshackle, fall-apart variety of devices that the young men had constructed in the village of Shuttlesworthing. Still, they felt awfully familiar.

While Dash whooped and danced back and forth in front of the performing monkeys, Flavia turned a corner of the gallery and lost her breath altogether.

A walnut tree grew out of the tiles, warm in sculpted bronze. It was bolted to the floor, and it was evident if you stepped close enough that every graceful branch and perfect leaf was made from metal. And yet...

It felt real. One of the miraculous engines was obviously at work at the heart of it, because a long sweep of fragile fronds moved slowly back and forth, catching imaginary breezes.

Silver nuts hung high in the branches, and one golden pear that looked good enough to bite into, just out of reach. "I had a little nut tree, nothing would it bear, but a silver nutmeg and a golden pear," Flavia whispered to herself.

This was ridiculous. She was a fairy, despite never having lived among her own people. There was no possible circumstance under which a man-made construction of a tree could affect her in this way. And yet she felt entirely seduced by the stirring of its branches, the rustle of its leaves. She might be standing on the edge of a river in her mother's country, inches away from dipping her foot into the cold water...

With a whirring sound, a cavity opened in the tree and a bright silver owl popped out, its beak flaring to hoot the hour. Music began to play, a silly music hall tune. Flavia pressed her hands to her mouth, laughing helplessly.

"Miss Wednesday?" called the distant voice of the Honourable Perrault Gloucester, somewhere in the outer hall. "I say, Miss Wednesday?"

Flavia winced. The thought of Perrault peering at this treasure through his lorgnette and pronouncing it a clever piece of rustic art or something equally banal made her want to scream.

Her eye fell upon the placard beside the extraordinary exhibit. It came as no particular surprise to read the names of ORLANDO AND RINALDO DEVICE, ROYAL ENGINEERS.

This fine example of artificial botany was created for Princess Ygraine on her sixteenth birthday, by commission of her Imperial Majesty, Queen Isolda. Legend has it that our Queen commissioned a small jewellery tree for her daughter's dressing table. The young royal engineers declared that, given the sheer

*amount of jewellery owned by the royal family, there
was little point to working in miniature.*

Flavia laughed again. That sounded like the gentlemen she knew.

The tree's mechanical boughs danced and weaved gently as the music wound to a close. Flavia reached up to touch a single leaf. Not quite knowing why, she slid the long, pale brown glove from her right arm — the arm made entirely of flowers and grasses and magic, the arm she wove for herself — and pressed her palm against the rough bronze bark of the tree.

For a moment, she felt entirely at peace.

The bronze warmed beneath her hand. The tree shivered. And a single word whispered up out of the leaves, a word that made Flavia's breath catch and her heart stutter.

"*Flaxenseed.*"

Not here. Not her.

Quicksilver.

Smooth twigs pricked at Flavia's wrists. Before she could move away, a branch wrapped itself entirely around her flowered forearm. She felt herself tugged in, and fell bodily against the uneven surface of the trunk. It smelled real. The stickiness of sap and freshness of the leaves filled her lungs. Ridiculous. It was bronze. "Let me go," she insisted.

"Flaxenseed," the tree moaned, Quicksilver's voice reverberating along its branches.

Oh, that voice. She had fallen in love with that

voice, before she even touched Quicksilver's hand, or saw her face. She had heard it in her dreams, had followed it down the winding paths to the Isle of Faerie. Her love, her lady of the greenwood, mocking and merry. Everything Flavia wanted. Everything Flavia wanted to be.

"Please..."

Quicksilver had never said 'please' a day in her life before, except perhaps to Tanaquil Gloriana, the Queen who commanded her entire loyalty.

"I am not listening to this." Flavia struggled against the branches and twigs that held her hard against the cool surface of the bronze tree. She flexed her magic flower hand, summoning what strength she had. "Leave me alone. I am not of her court anymore, *I gave you up*. Let me go."

The branches wrapped around her waist, pulling her even more intimately against the tree trunk. Caressing her thighs, her hips, with knotted bronze. She could feel Quicksilver's leafy breath against her cheek. Quicksilver was the loveliest of the queen's court, and the sharpest. Her mother's Hand and Voice.

How Flavia had longed for her to touch her like this, once upon a time. How she had thrilled at every caress of her hand.

Quicksilver hated her now. Flavia knew that from the night on the banks of the lake in the Forest of Arden. Flavia turned against the queen, and Quicksilver broke her arm. There was no love left between them, no softness, not even in the memory of the past.

How we danced.

Quicksilver was always better at pretending to be Flavia's friend than the others. She had kept it up even after Tanaquil Gloriana no longer demanded it. As Flavia's dreams about that other world shifted from the innocent play of childhood to something more wild and wanton, Quicksilver was at the centre of her desires.

Flavia's first kiss was at a Midsummer dance, with a faery lady all masked in apple blossom. It was not Quicksilver's usual true face of ivy leaves, but Flavia had recognised her hands and her merry eyes. Her kiss had heated Flavia all the way to her toes.

Quicksilver was not hers. Had never been hers. She served one woman with her heart and that was the Queen of Faerie, not her wayward, traitorous daughter.

"Flaxenseed," Quicksilver whispered now through the tree trunk, teasing her hair with bronze twigs and branches, tugging at the tight braided bun. "It is not too late. You can still free us. Be our champion. Be our treasure."

"I made my choice," Flavia said flatly.

"You have driven your mother mad. She will kill us all, trapped here as we are. Help us. Free us from her wrath."

With a flick of one bronze branch, and then another, Quicksilver stripped Flavia of her other glove.

Several buttons rolled free on the floor as the tree dangled the sleeve of brown silk high above her head, then flung it out of reach.

Flavia called upon her own magic. She shoved her bare grass-and-clover arm hard against the bronze trunk and pushed a burst of summer sunshine directly into the metal so as to propel herself away, out of Quicksilver's grasp. Her flesh arm blushed green, taking on its natural colour. "Leave me alone!" she gasped.

"Miss Wednesday!" she heard Perrault call again, closer than before. By instinct, Flavia shoved her magic back down inside her, returning pink and white to her skin so fast that it burned hot and angry.

The ends of her hair were still tangled in the branches, and she dared not come nearer to release herself. Quicksilver was silent. "In here, my lord!" Flavia cried out. Embarrassing, that she needed to be rescued.

Dash reached her first, his feet pattering across the floor. "What happened, Miss Wednesday?"

"Don't touch the branches," Flavia instructed him, not wanting Quicksilver to have access to the boy. "Pass me a glove, quick!"

Dash tossed her one of her brown gloves so that she could slide it over the botanical mess of stalks and flowers that formed her false arm. He asked no questions, which made her think that he remembered more than she had realised, about that night in the Forest of Arden.

"Heavens," said Perrault, entering the hall a moment later at an unhurried saunter. "Are you quite all right, Miss Wednesday?"

"A bit of a predicament, I'm afraid," Flavia said, managing a small laugh. "Could you possibly..."

"Why yes, indeed." She felt his hands touching her hair. "I'm afraid I might have to — oh, dear." The bone pins she used to keep her coiffure tidy scattered to the ground, ringing on the floorboards.

"It's fine," Flavia said. She made herself breathe gently, becoming the calm governess once again. "Please, as quick as you can." The tree hissed behind her. "Ow!"

"Your hair looks funny," noted Dash, handing Flavia her other glove. Deftly, he poured the stray buttons into her cupped hand.

"Hush, you," said Queenie, watching the whole business from a distance. When Flavia glanced up at her, the young lady's eyes looked knowing.

Perrault freed Flavia's hair. She moved away from the bronze branch with relief, catching Dash's hand to pull him with her, to a safe distance beside Queenie. "Thank you, sir," Flavia said, regaining her composure as best she could.

To her dismay, the young aristocrat was leaning into the bronze tree, his hands pressed carelessly against one of the branches as he examined the trunk. "Such a fine piece," he muttered to himself. "Extraordinary. Ingenious. One might almost say... miraculous."

"I do not think you should touch it, sir," Flavia said, keeping her voice low and calm. She wanted to scream at him to get away, but one did not scream at a peer's son if one wanted him to listen and follow advice.

She had learned a lot about gentlemen during her time in service.

"Ah, yes," said Perrault. He stepped smartly back from the tree and pushed his spectacles further up his nose. "If we hurry, we should have time to peruse the clockwork engine exhibit, and the kinescopes, before we stop at the tea rooms."

"I want a cake!" said Dash. This was his standard interjection, heard several times a day. Right now, it was entirely welcome.

"That sounds like an excellent plan," said Flavia, tidying her hair as best she could without crawling on the floor to recover her lost pins. She did not want to get close to that tree again for any reason. She tucked the stray buttons into her reticule, and lifted her bosom high. *Good posture covers a magnitude of ills*, Miss Troughton used to say to the girls of the School of Good Wives and God's Mercy.

If Quicksilver wanted to go around haunting bronze trees, she could jolly well haunt this one for as long as she liked. By evening, Flavia and the Gloucester children would be back safe in their home, surrounded by the iron-clad lamp posts and railings of London.

As Perrault led the children on through the Crystal Palace, Flavia's thoughts turned to Rinaldo and Orlando Device. Was it a coincidence that it was *their* tree that Quicksilver had possessed so readily?

She resigned herself to an afternoon of busy thoughts and sore feet as they perambulated around the many wonders of the Exhibition.

Flavia had escaped Quicksilver, had survived her attack, and proved herself resilient to her old love's blandishments. That was something to be proud of. Before the afternoon was over, there would be tea and cake.

Things were looking up.

1845 - *Anna Russell, the Duchess of Bedford, is credited with the invention of a light meal of cakes and sandwiches alongside a cup of Darjeeling, to cure "a certain sinking feeling" one might suffer in the mid-afternoon.*

— Titania Raspbridge, *A Timeline of High Tea in Britannia* (2024)

Chapter 5

In Which a Nursery Tea is Not All That It Seems

The London house had no schoolroom, and so
Flavia's lessons were conducted in the Earl's
library, an elegant room of pomegranate-and-
cress wallpaper and green leather chairs.

It was lucky that she had been given free use of this
room during the day, as the shelves laden with prettily-
matched volumes were more orderly than those at
Gloucester Worth, and thefts might be readily
apparent.

Indeed, the library was so surprised and pleased to
have visitors that its shelves practically tipped useful
volumes into Flavia's arms as she and the children
passed by. There were remarkably few works on magic
in the collection, certainly nothing as advanced as one
might expect from Lady Mortmain's supposed magical
prowess.

Clearly, the enchantress' real library of practical

texts was elsewhere in the house, which explained why this room was so neglected.

On the day after the excursion to the Winter Exhibition, Flavia returned to her usual curriculum, with mixed results. Trying to teach mathematics to Dash on a good day was like trying to teach table manners to a monkey. The first two hours of this particular morning had been exactly like that, as he refused to take any shape other than that of a small gibbon.

Queenie was supposed to be practicing her handwriting by copying a text out on to writing paper, with ink and quill. Flavia had hoped to please her by finding a treatise on the application of culinary science to love philtres (with reference to why such potions were more easily concealed in sugary rather than salty foods). The task held little interest for the young alchemist. Whenever she thought her governess was not looking, Queenie would switch books and read up on the various theories of practical invisibility instead.

Finally Flavia gave in and allowed Dash to draw pictures of his favourite feats of engineering from yesterday's excursion, on condition that he retain the shape of a human boy for at least an hour.

This allowed her to get on with some study of her own. Back in the library at Gloucester Worth, Flavia had located a thick tome of legends from the Age of Chivalry, and packed it in her clothes trunk to bring along to the London House. Amongst its many tales of hapless knights and sinister enchantresses, there were plentiful references to the Forest of Arden. Nearly every story involved the drinking of a philtre from the wrong enchanted fountain, and the search for another fountain to undo the damage that the first had caused. Not to mention a great deal of non-consensual kissing, marrying and suchlike.

Flavia found herself making notes concerning the philtres natural to the Forest:

- Fountain of Love (*features in all the stories, is there more than one or is it just conveniently placed?*)
- Fountain of Love-me-not (*antidote to the former*)
- Fountain of Hate (*also surprisingly popular in the tales: enemies-to-lovers is such a popular trope*)
- Fountain of Truth (*less common except when the writer of tales clearly wishes to resolve their story abruptly*)
- Fountain of Life (*surprisingly scanty references, surely this one would be most convenient!*)
- Fountain of Wisdom (*entirely absent from most of these romances*)
- Fountain of Know-not (*not an antidote to Wisdom, though one story suggests that Wisdom can be used as an antidote to Know-not – check this in various sources*)

- Fountain of Oblivion (*terrifying*)
- Fountain of Youth (*not as appealing as one might think, but a solid motivation for villains*)
- Fountain of Transformation (*always with "hilarious" results*)
- Fountain of Undoing (*exceptionally useful! Why is this not in every enchanter's back pocket?? Surely would be useful when the Love-Me-Not runs out if nothing else*)
- Fountain of the Water of Worlds (*?????*)

No wonder that the knights and enchantresses of those stories were all so confused! They were at various times combining up to four philtres simply to function in everyday life.

Flavia now understood why the Forest of Arden had been deemed so dangerous that it was closed off from humanity after the Faerie were exiled to their island.

What did Lady Mortmain want with the Forest's bounty of magical philtres? Could she have the same motivation as Queenie: a desire to restore the family's fortune by gaining access to the waters of the Fountain of Love-Me-Not? It seemed unlikely that the answer was that simple — not when there was power to be had from the other fountains as well.

Queenie was not going to forget the promise that Flavia had made on that terrible night, to escort the girl back into the Forest of Arden at the next solstice. The more Flavia read of the Forest's disreputable history, the more she fretted about the dangers of that journey.

Today, she was so engrossed in her book that she did not notice Perrault entering the library. He leaned against the door frame with a casual indolence that did not match his usual demeanour.

"I'm sorry, sir," said Flavia, jumping slightly. "I did not see you there. Do you require the children, or the library?"

"Neither," he said with a slow smile. "I want you, Miss Wednesday." When she did not immediately answer, he crooked his finger.

Reluctantly, Flavia set down her book and informed Queenie and Dash that she would be back shortly. "How can I help you, sir?" she asked politely in the relative privacy of the empty corridor.

Perrault reached out and closed the library door firmly behind her, removing witnesses to their encounter.

His eyes were brighter than usual, and he spoke in a deliberate manner. "I have a message from my sister-in-law, Elspeth." He was standing far too close. Flavia attempted to slide sideways, and found herself backing into the wall. "Tea."

"Tea?" Flavia repeated stupidly. Had Perrault's eyes always been that colour? There was a silver light to them that was strangely mesmerising. The last thing she needed was to be caught gazing into the eyes of the young master of the house like a love-struck parlour maid. She blinked, several times. "But Lady Mortmain pays calls in the mornings."

Perrault smiled, an entirely different smile to anything she had seen upon his face before. He looked... hungry. "This afternoon. Four o'clock. She wishes to take tea with the children, and hear all about their adventure at the Winter Exhibition."

There had been ample opportunities to discuss the excursion at supper yesterday, and breakfast this morning. Flavia was certain that every anecdote that Dash and Queenie could summon between them had been shared already, so determined were they to convince their father he had been right to send them. Lady Mortmain was present on both occasions, and it seemed unlikely she was anxious to hear more.

Still, it was none of Flavia's business if the lady of the house chose to have tea with her nephew and niece. "I will send them along at four o'clock," she said evenly.

Perrault moved nearer, close enough to dance with her.

How do I escape if he wants to kiss me? she thought wretchedly. Her grass-and-flowers arm twitched beneath its glove, reminding her that she was a magical creature, and not without defences. But Flavia dared not use magic in the house of an enchantress, not if she wanted to stay concealed.

"And you," Perrault said in a low voice.

Flavia blinked at him, feeling stupid. "Lady Mortmain wishes me to join the children for tea?"

"Oh yes." The young lord lingered too near for her to misconstrue the threat of his intent. Finally, he stepped back, putting a far more appropriate distance between them as if he had never taken such a liberty. "I shall escort you, Miss Wednesday. At four o'clock."

"There's no need," Flavia said sharply. It was so much easier to breathe with two feet of empty air between them. But she could not feel relief, not now she knew he was a danger to her. "It's only downstairs."

Perrault's face crinkled up into another of those strange smiles. "Ah, but it's all about appearances, Miss Wednesday. Is it not? Everything should be done correctly."

He turned on his heel and walked swiftly away, leaving Flavia feeling as if she had evaded an elaborate trap.

Or, indeed, had fallen into one.

～

Rinaldo slept.
Rinaldo woke.
Rinaldo dreamed.

Rinaldo dreamed of bronze, warm beneath his hands, of water pouring back and forth. He dreamed of his magic, and Orlando's magic, surging against each other like waves, but never quite touching.

Rinaldo dreamed of the look on Princess Ygraine's face as her wedding fell into chaos around her.

Rinaldo slept.

Rinaldo woke.

Rinaldo dreamed.

Lady Elspeth Mortmain hosted tea in a beautiful sage-green parlour featuring a delicate ivy-patterned wallpaper, in intricate swirls. Every surface overflowed with potted plants, green and leafy. The air was sweet with the scent of earth and growing.

It was the first time that the lady had shown any inclination to spend time with the children outside of breakfast, luncheon and supper.

The Honourable Perrault, true to his word, escorted Flavia, Queenie and Dash from the library to the parlour, then gave a polite bow before leaving them to it. Flavia was relieved, as she had been half expecting a cup to be set out for him as well. This situation was awkward enough.

Mr Graves waited upon them with his usual earnest dignity. The butler of Number 12 looked so similar to the butler of Gloucester Worth that Flavia had spent the first three days half convinced he was the same person, though it had been explained to her that this was the father of her Mr Graves, who was referred to in this household as Mr Graves the Younger.

The table was laid with the finest porcelain teaset, paper thin with a pattern of peonies in springtime. The lovely cups and saucers were joined by an exquisite spread of bite-sized cakes, slivered sandwiches, and enticing fragrances.

As Flavia took her seat between Queenie and Dash, it occurred to her that there was something very important she should remember about Lady Mortmain, something she should keep at the forefront of her mind. Something to do with the Forest of Arden, perhaps? But the rich odours from the tea, and the crusty cinnamon of the miniature apple sponges, pushed all worry out of her head.

"I do love being an Aunt, Miss Wednesday," Lady Mortmain confided as if they were the greatest of friends. She poured tea all around, with extra milk and sugar for the children, and slices of lemon for herself and Flavia. "All the joys of the little dears, birthday parcels and tiny frocks and such treats, but none of the drudgery. I do not envy my sister's burden, what with the marriage market to deal with, and all those social pitfalls she must avoid to ensure Petronella and Dash-mond are properly settled."

Flavia could not take her eyes off the beautiful figure of Lady Mortmain. She had known the lady was attractive, but never felt it quite so intensely before. Her hair glowed like golden sunlight, and she gazed at

Flavia — a humble governess — as if she, too, was lovely. She wore a pearl brooch upon a lilac gown that set off her complexion to perfection. She smelled of roses and leaves trodden underfoot and acorns and all things that were good. When she breathed, her breasts rose and fell like perfect loaves of yeasted dough.

Dashmond was doing what all boys liked best to do at a formal tea, which was experimenting with how many cakes he could fit in his mouth all at once before an adult told him he should stop.

Queenie could be relied upon to play the proper lady in public, nibbling on sandwiches and pretending not to care about the cakes (well, perhaps just one or two). Like her brother, she was not remotely engaged with what her Aunt was saying.

Flavia had no idea what Lady Mortmain was saying either. The part of her that paid attention to such things had floated dreamily out of the window. Lady Mortmain's voice was so melodious that the actual content of her conversation did not matter in the least. Flavia could listen to that sensuous voice all day.

She wondered if it might be appropriate to lean in, and lick Lady Mortmain's neck. What was the proper etiquette concerning ladies licking other ladies at a formal tea?

There was something not quite proper about that thought, but she did not have the attention span to interrogate it. This tea was delicious.

A spindly yellow cat, the same shade as Lady

Carolinge's sallow furnishings back at Gloucester Worth, sat on the window sill, its tail swishing back and forth. While Lady Mortmain said clever things about the Age of Chivalry, which related to the book Flavia had recently been reading, Flavia's attention was finally drawn away, to the cat with its clever, jewel-like eyes.

The cat was not nearly so appealing as the delicious scent of Lady Mortmain's skin. Elspeth. Dare Flavia call her Elspeth?

"But of course, the Forest of Arden is just a story," said Elspeth now, her voice strumming attractively.

Delighted to make a useful contribution to the conversation, Flavia opened her mouth to say that no, it was not just a story, as she and the children had been there quite recently.

A sharp sensation stopped her. Queenie had kicked her, under the table. What an odd thing for her to do!

Elspeth passed a plate of heart-shaped lemon shortbreads. Flavia took one, which crumbled delicately on her tongue, carrying a hint of bitterness along with the sweet.

Despite the faces that Queenie continued to pull for no apparent reason, Flavia opened her mouth, and spoke. It all poured out of her, so desperate was she to please Lady Elspeth. She told her of the hours they had spent in the Forest of Arden, only a few weeks earlier. Of the lake and the fountains, of the topiary and the confrontation with the Queen of the Fairies, and of course the Extraordinary and Miraculous Device Brothers. It was so kind of Lady Elspeth to take such an interest.

As Flavia talked, her head and eyelids became heavier. The last thing she was aware of before she finally fell into a deep slumber was the amused eyes of the yellow cat and its swishing, swishing tail.

～

Coldness awoke her, a harsh shock of freezing wet. Flavia blinked to find herself sitting on the floor of the nursery, drenched in water. Queenie stood over her, holding the empty water jug from her basin, the china one with peach-coloured roses and daisies painted upon it.

Flavia could taste aniseed on her tongue. "Is that —" she murmured.

"An antidote philtre," snapped Queenie. "It's specific to Aunt Elspeth's magics. I brewed it when I was nine, after realising how often she enchanted me to spill Mother's secrets to her. They boil up into a rather effective lozenge. I ate one before we went to tea."

"I wish I had," Flavia sighed. Her head ached badly. "Goodness, what did I tell her?"

"Everything," said the young girl sternly. "About the night of All Hallows, and how Dash and I let you in through the gate, and those two nice Device gentlemen, and..."

Worse than she had imagined. Flavia cradled her forehead in her hands. "And my mother," she whispered. "Did she ask about my mother?"

Queenie nodded. "They're old friends, apparently. She asked if your mother had a spy in her house, because Aunt Elspeth has one in hers. You didn't know, so I suppose at least you couldn't tell her that."

"*I'm* the spy," Flavia groaned. "At least I was supposed to be, back at Gloucester Worth. I can't think how my mother would have arranged any others, unless she is willing and able to hire mortals, somehow." She accepted the towel that Queenie offered, and dried herself off as best she could. "Where's Dash?"

"Setting up a toy train in the library. I thought it would keep him splendidly busy while we had a chance to talk about *important things*."

"Good idea." Still damp, Flavia sat gingerly on the edge of Queenie's bed. "If your aunt has a spy in my mother's house, if one of the fairies really works for her, then that's good news. I mean, that suggests that they're not working together. It could have been the spy, and not my mother who informed Lady Mortmain I was going to open the gateway to the Forest of Arden on All Hallows, so she knew to send through the Device brothers at the same time."

Queenie frowned. "I'm not sure it's better to have a

Faerie Queen and a powerful enchantress working against us separately, rather than together."

"It might be better for us, if they work against each other," said Flavia. "Though they can certainly cause a great deal of harm to us, either way." How could she have let her guard down so badly? She had forgotten that this house was enemy territory.

It was just so *lovely*.

She considered what other information she might have provided to Lady Mortmain. "Did she know that you and Dash were the key to the gate, before I spoke?"

"I don't think so," said Queenie. "She got quite furious when you mentioned that, and smashed a chocolate eclair with her teacup. After tea, she went straight to Father. I overheard her suggesting to him that Dash and I stay here with her a while after he and Mother return home. And you, I suppose. Since you're our governess."

Flavia could not believe she had been such a fool. Why had she not thought to avoid a situation where Lady Mortmain would be able to feed her cakes? "We must decide what to do," she said, feeling hollow inside. Had the cakes even been real? She rather thought her stomach was full of sawdust.

Queenie frowned. "If Dash and I need to run away in a hurry, will you come with us?"

She seemed to consider Flavia as more of an ally than her aunt, at least. That in turn suggested Queenie might be close to forgiving Flavia for the betrayal of All Hallows.

"Yes," Flavia said at once, then thought about what she had said. "You mustn't run away without me. If your aunt has plans for your future, then you're safe here for the time being."

Queenie nodded. "I agree. But it's best to have options."

Flavia moaned. There was a painful thumping sensation behind her eyes. "Do you have any lozenges for a headache?"

"Not this one. You earned that headache. Get some sleep. There's nothing to be done for now." Queenie led Flavia to her bed in the dressing room beside the nursery — a governess had been an afterthought in the transportation of the household, with no space reserved for her among the London servants — and tucked a blanket around her as if Flavia were the child. "Shall I make some more Auntidotes?"

Flavia laughed despite her aching head. A perfect name for a useful lozenge. "Yes please," she said. "We're going to need them if we're to get anything done around here."

If only she had had such magical protection at All Hallows when she faced her mother, she might still have both of her arms.

～

R inaldo slept.

Rinaldo woke.

Rinaldo dreamed of a house that hated him, of molten bronze pouring from room to room, shaping wall sconces and textured carpet and wallpaper covered in peonies, pomegranates, pimpernels.

Rinaldo dreamed of patterns pressed into bronze, of water cold on his tongue, of magic, magic, always magic.

Sometimes he reached out as he awoke, always dreading that his brother would be gone, manacles hanging empty.

But no. When he awoke, Orlando was always there, snoring beside him, chains tangled around his wrist. Apple blossom was sprouting from them. A ladybird had taken up residence on Orlando's left wrist.

The ankle chains were willow fronds, tight and impossible to escape.

Rinaldo woke, and stared at the wallpaper. Clover leaves and cornflowers.

"Orlando?" he murmured, stretching his hands. They felt tired, as if the work he had been doing in his sleep had carried over to his body.

What work have I been doing?

"Orlando," he said again. "Have I been here, all this time? Did I go somewhere?"

"Shhh," murmured his brother. "Sleeping now."

Rinaldo slept. He dreamed of warm bronze, and a house that hated him.

~

Flavia slept deeply for several hours, and then sat bolt upright, alone in a dark room.

It was the middle of the night. In a huge house like this, with its creaking and silences, there was no mistaking it.

She could hear the light breathing of Queenie and Dash, asleep themselves, in the nursery. At least they could be together again, here in the townhouse.

Something green shone out of the darkness. Cat's eyes.

It was an odd creature for Lady Mortmain to keep — hardly one of the fluffy house pets that usually adorned a wealthy house. It had a lean and hungry look to it, with yellow fur almost as visible in the dark as its jewel-bright eyes.

"There's no point in spying on me for your mistress," Flavia said tartly. "She's eaten all my secrets, and washed them down with tea."

The cat leaped from the foot of her bed and landed on the floor, then padded to the doorway, nudging it further open with its nose. It stared at her with an air of expectation.

"Oh no," Flavia whispered. "You won't catch me chasing a cat around *this* house in the middle of the night. Not with Lady Elspeth on the warpath, and every room half in love with her."

The cat sniffed, and walked away.

Flavia followed. Of course she did. At least she was still wearing her day dress. Midnight adventures were bad enough without wandering around in one's night-rail like something out of a Gothic novel.

The humble memory charm is second only to the love philtre in popularity. While the memory charm's origins lie in the long-lost River of Lethe, and Lethe's cousin (the Fountain of Oblivion from the Forest of Arden), modern human manufacture has replaced them both with commonplace spellcraft. Unlike the love philtre, there is no known antidote for a memory charm, largely because the human brain contains natural defences against such magics.

Repeated use may, however, cause long-lasting effects.

— The Encyclopedia of Magic, 1814 edition.

Chapter 6

In Which Following a Cat in the Night-time has Surprising Consequences

The yellow cat was clearly aware that Flavia was following. It chose the the servant's stairs, rather than taking her out to the main staircase.

There was something very strange about the way it moved. She could not say that she was an expert on felines, but those she had seen before moved like they were made of water and fur and silk, all smooth purr on legs. This creature had that aspect down most of the time, but on the stairs it had a strange, jerky motion to its gait.

As if it was not a cat at all. Frankly, considering the meaningful looks it kept throwing her way, this was something of a relief.

The cat led the way down and down, into the lower corridors and all the way to the kitchen door. Warmth and light poured out of the doorway; it was late enough for even the servants to be abed, but someone was still here. Flavia hesitated on the stairs, then peeked in to see Perrault sitting near the kitchen fire, being treated to tea and fruitcake by Mrs Brundage.

This was the one thing she liked about him: that he had such an easy relationship with the cook who had worked in this house since he was a child. But that was before his sinister behaviour today. How much did he know of what Lady Elspeth had planned for Flavia and the children? Had he been listening all the while Flavia spilled her secrets in a haze of sugared biscuits?

Here in the kitchen, he appeared his usual self, smiling at Mrs Brundage's chatter and sipping at his cup of tea. The fruitcake lay uneaten on a saucer in his lap, which was unusual. But of course, the family had dined well this evening. They always did. Enough courses for a fairy revel that lasted all day. So much food; so much largesse.

"I know you wouldn't lie to me, Master Perry," the cook said as she kneaded bread dough for tomorrow.

"Upon my word, Mrs Brundage," he assured her. "I have no more idea than you what is happening in the cellar."

"Oh, I have an idea, all right," she said, tutting at him. "We all have an idea, don't we? Her ladyship's gone and taken prisoners again. The notice-not charm leaves a lemon scent in the air, and why else would my flour and hams smell of citrus at this time of year? Not to mention all the crashing and banging that shakes up my blessed kitchen every time one of them tries to escape. I had to bake three sponge cakes this morning. The first two were ruined thanks to vibrations from Down There."

Perrault placed his cup and plate back on the table, an entirely insincere expression of sympathy on his face. "It's a scandal, what you have to deal with, Mrs B."

"Don't get me wrong," the cook said quickly. "I love our mistress dearly, she's been good to me, and to all of us below stairs. She's just not one for remembering that them that works for her has ears and brains for ourselves." She added a slap of flour to her dough. "It's no skin off my nose if she wants to keep forty prisoners down there, I'm sure she has her reasons. It's the pretence I've no time for."

"You're a busy woman," Perrault agreed in a bored drawl. "All you ask is a little respect."

The cook was supposed to know him well; could she not tell that something was amiss with the gentleman? Or perhaps he always behaved like this in London, and Flavia had never got the measure of him before now.

"...And I could do without those memory charms she slaps on me after sending me down to feed the poor mites she has chained up in the cellar, and all," complained the cook. "It does my head in, having to keep track of all my meal plans and grocery orders with part of the day's thoughts missing from my head. It's insulting, that's what it is."

Flavia drew back from the kitchen doorway. The yellow cat glared balefully at her. "No," she whispered. "I can see quite clearly that you meant me to overhear that, and that you intend me to go and investigate these prisoners in the cellar. I'm not going to do it. My only responsibility in this house is to the children, and we are in enough trouble without poking our nose into whatever else Lady Mortmain is cooking up. It's none of my business."

Bad enough that this house was run by an enchantress with sinister designs on her own niece and nephew. Now there was a cat who could predict conversations in kitchens? Flavia did not like this at all.

The yellow cat continued to gaze at her as she backed away.

"Don't give me that," she hissed. "You are *not* the one paying my wages. I absolutely, categorically refuse to follow the non-verbal instructions of an enchantress's house pet."

The cat looked away only once, to stare meaningfully at the lamps that hung in sconces along the corridor wall, and then in the direction of a staircase that could only lead to the cellar.

"Oh, for goodness sake," said Flavia.

~

Rinaldo woke.

It had been weeks, yes? More than days. It was so hard to tell.

The most worrying aspect was the time lapses. He was certain that their food was regularly dosed with memory charms. Other spells as well, he imagined.

He might convince Orlando to skip a meal or two to test his theory, but he did not recall eating anything since they arrived. His belly always felt sated. Hard to go on a hunger strike when you were eating in your sleep — or in some other drugged condition you could not recall.

On the rare occasion he was able to drag Orlando's attention away from his latest disastrous magical escape attempt, it was clear that his brother had corresponding gaps in his own memory.

Being chained to a wall was tiring and painful, and yet neither of them were in as bad shape as Rinaldo might have predicted. They must be getting some kind of exercise which they did not recall. He believed that during many of these holes in his memory, his magic had been similarly exercised.

Rinaldo had held back from using his magic in the cellar, except for the occasional droplets he allowed his brother to borrow for his escape plans. Going for weeks without properly releasing the sparks in his system should have his body in rebellion. He should be ready to explode, his limp fingers summoning every teaspoon and garden rake and pin in this house.

But Rinaldo's magic remained quiet, as sated as his belly. Either the enchantress was stealing it from him in some way, wringing him out like a sponge, or... he was employing it himself, and did not remember the circumstances.

Orlando grew more and more inventive with his attempts to escape the bonds placed upon them by the enchantress. Every time he tried, some new layer of her magic would unravel to stop him.

His manacles-and-chain had been daisy chains for some days: before that they were variously rope, spiky rose stalks, snakes, and on one particularly distressing afternoon, a dark tar that oozed out of the walls and engulfed not only Orlando's wrists, but his entire body.

Rinaldo's own chains were largely left alone, though sometimes the latest counter-spell would affect him too, for the hell of it. That at least gave he and his brother an opportunity to yell at each other for a while, which was somewhat satisfying.

Rinaldo broke his own 'no unnecessary magic' rule to transform a teaspoon into a rudimentary lock pick which at least had kept Orlando quiet for a few days, if 'quiet' meant 'bringing even more magical defences down upon his head.'

"She's using us for something," Rinaldo told Orlando. "She wants us alive and working on some diabolic project of hers. Considering that our speciality is creating giant automata out of household metals, do you think we should be concerned?"

To which Orlando replied: "If I could just find the right substance to transform these chains into before the counter spell kicks in... did I try milk already?" which showed he wasn't really listening.

During his darker hours, Rinaldo considered how stupid they had been to return here, expecting Lady Mortmain to keep her promise and reward them for their quest into Arden. It was clear she did not want them free to tell the world about her secrets.

If only they had stayed in that bloody tavern. It was not often that Rinaldo could mark a point where their lives would have trod a better path if they had only drunk *more* on a particular night, but he wished he was there at Samson's place now, carousing stupidly with his brother and never once thinking about the mess they had made of things with Queen Isolda, and her daughter.

(*Ygraine.* What had happened to her after that mess of a wedding? Rinaldo wished he could take it all back, apologise. Most of all, he wished that when he and Orlando fled the palace, they had not taken the damned cat with them, and dropped it straight into the hands of Lady Mortmain.)

They could have made a run for it, after All Hallows. Could have taken the philtres Orlando stole from the fountains, and used them to fund a trip across the ocean to Vienna, or Egypt. Even India.

Rinaldo's country of origin might be ruled by Queen Isolda's viceroys, but surely her wrath could not extend across the entire land. Rinaldo was so sick of fighting to belong in *this* wretched country with its rain and its arrogant aristocrats, and that surprised expression most white people displayed when they heard the upper class Britannian accent he had learned from a decade living as a curiosity in a palace.

He was even sick of his name, a stolen conceit from a fairy story. His name was Orlando's fault. Everything was Orlando's fault.

Rinaldo had learned at an early age that wherever he went there would always be Britannians who thought it reasonable to treat him poorly because of his dark hair, skin, eyes. It infuriated him now to remember how accepting he had been of that — a quiet child, who wanted nothing more than to spend his life fixing things.

As Rinaldo Device, Royal Engineer, he had enjoyed the greatest and best 'fixing things' job that the Empire could possibly have to offer. With the Queen's patronage, he and Orlando had both benefited from being seen as exotic and fashionable instead of suspicious foreigners. The world had offered itself up on a plate for Rinaldo and Orlando Device... for a while.

There was no recapturing that, no possible redemption. Not even if they dipped the cat in gold and presented it on a diamond plate.

Not if they knelt at the feet of Princess Ygraine and begged for her forgiveness.

Rinaldo could not begin to imagine who he might be without the fancy suits, top hats and grand reputation of the Extraordinary and Miraculous Device Brothers: engineers and metallurmages to the Crown. He was not that shy and terrified child from the Worthy Orphans any more, the boy who had disappeared in Buckingham Palace and become someone quite new.

He was not Rajendra, orphan of no last name, no history, no family. He would not want to be that boy again. But what remained?

What would he even do, in India? He would be a stranger, lost in a land full of strangers. Here, at least, in Britannia he knew what to be afraid of.

Enchantresses, mostly.

Everything had bled out of him here in this cellar: purpose, hunger, ambition. Everything except his anger. He wanted to hate Orlando for how it had all turned out, but their downfall was like their magic. Equally owned by them both.

Orlando sang quietly under his breath. It was one of those things he did when he was bored. Clearly, the lockpick had lost its mystique. Rinaldo looked across at his brother, who had been irritating him for their entire imprisonment, and found himself smiling, despite it all.

At least neither of them were alone.

He might change his mind if Orlando was still

singing the same song half an hour from now, but for now Rinaldo had his company to be grateful for.

A brother was the best gift he had ever been given; the best thing he had ever taken for himself.

"Cat," said Orlando suddenly, breaking into Rinaldo's train of thought. "Look. It's that bloody cat, come to taunt us again. Do you have a brick to turf at him?"

"No," said Rinaldo, yawning and stretching his arms as much as he was able. "Also, that's probably treason."

"I'd swap the Tower of London for this cellar any day of the week. We know we can escape from *there*. Hey, cat!" Orlando yelled. "You ruined our lives, do you know that, arsehole?"

The yellow cat leaped nimbly on to the bannister, content with any life-ruining he may or may not be responsible for.

"Someone else is coming," Rinaldo whispered. He heard footsteps on the stairs, saw the glow of a lamp.

"If it's that bitch Lady Mortmain, she ruined our lives too," said Orlando. "OH, YES, YOU DID, MADAM. With your pouty lips and your golden hair and a most impressive figure for a lady of your age…"

"I don't think it is her," said Rinaldo in a low voice. "Which might be for the best considering that crack about her age."

A sturdy figure in a long dress stepped into view, barely lit by the lamp she held, which was barely brighter than the one that had been left to them, burning oil in the corner. She frowned, staring around the cellar, and Rinaldo's heart sank as he recognised her round, thoughtful face. He would know that chin anywhere.

The fairy governess, braided hair coiled up into a snood, her arms covered with long gloves to hide the fact that one of those arms was made of woven grass and random wildflowers.

She swung her lamp from side to side, peering around as if there were nothing more interesting in front of her than a stack of rice bags. Damn it all: the notice-not charm was as effective on her as it had been on the servants.

"Miss Wednesday," Rinaldo groaned. "She can't see or hear us."

"So, get her attention," Orlando insisted.

"That's not exactly my speciality."

"Try," insisted his brother. "I've been saying you should get more practice talking to girls. Start with this one."

~

S o much for the cat's interference. There were no prisoners in this cellar.

Flavia looked around the place, shivering. The air tasted of metal and misery. Whatever Lady Mortmain had been doing down here, among the ham hocks and the flour barrels, it was far from good.

Her skin buzzed irritably, as if eight different kinds of charm were fighting each other, with no care for who got splattered by the rebound. "There's no one here," Flavia told the cat. "I'm going back to bed before I get into even more trouble."

She should not have risked leaving the nursery. She needed to stay near the children at all times. She did not know if Lady Mortmain's plans for them were short or long term.

The yellow cat made a noise. It was not a noise one usually associated with a cat. It opened its mouth wider, and a mechanical clank-whirr emanated from beyond its very pink tongue.

Flavia hesitated. "What did you say?" she ventured. At least no one was here to see her being stupid.

The cat clanked again. It shuddered, vibrated, and hawked up three silver teaspoons as if they were hairballs.

Flavia blinked in astonishment. "You do not make the convincing argument that you intend," she told the cat sternly. "Good night."

Very slowly, the teaspoons each stood up on their ends. As Flavia watched, the teaspoons jiggled and danced a little, then balanced carefully one on top of each other. The yellow cat turned away in boredom, making it clear that it had nothing to do with such hijinks.

"Oh," Flavia breathed. "It is you, after all. I might

have known." She swept her gaze and then her lamp back over the cellar. This time, she paid particular attention to the empty wall that was screaming at her not to notice it, not to bother. *Nothing to see here, turn around and wander away...*

It was wallpapered. The entire cellar was wallpapered in a beautiful, tangled pattern of cornflowers and clover leaves, Who would choose such pretty wallpaper for a cellar?

She stepped very deliberately forward, one slow step at a time until she was barely two feet from the empty wall. "Mr Device? And Mr Device?"

She could feel it now, the notice-not spell, spread from wall to wall like a bedsheet. The sparks shivered against her as she reached out to touch the illusion of nothingness. Notice-not was a form of illusion, and Flavia had always been very good with illusion. She had been wearing one for most of her life, just to appear human.

She could smell rose petals now, an overwhelming perfume, and lemon. The trick was to be gentle, so very gentle that Lady Mortmain did not sense her spells being tampered with. Flavia breathed in, and out. On the third inhalation, she snipped the notice-not spell free and breathed it deeply into her own lungs.

She held her breath, blinked, and found herself staring into a pair of dark, dancing eyes. She faced the ridiculously beautiful Mr Orlando Device, far too close for comfort. Close enough for dancing. His hair was in a most scurrilous state, messier than she had even seen it before.

Orlando smiled at her with so much dazzling charm that the sun all but came out, right there in the cellar. "Hello there, my knight in shining armour," he proclaimed.

"Our knight in shining armour," interrupted his grumpy brother, who stood nearby. He rattled his chains against the wall, for emphasis.

"That too," said Orlando Device.

She had found the prisoners. Flavia exhaled, and let exactly half of the broken spell return to the air around them.

"What on earth am I going to do with you two?" she said aloud.

"Come," said Fairy Harebell with a merry twinkle. "Let us dance the fairy circle, to make the toadstools grow beneath our feet. And then we shall share a picnic."

"A picnic!" gasped Margaret, eyes as wide as buttercups. "What sort of picnic?"

"Why, all the best things to eat and drink. Dancing makes the food taste nicer."

"I don't know how to dance," said Cedric, who hoped there would be sausage rolls.

Fairy Harebell took his hand. "Everyone can dance! Once the music plays, your feet won't be able to help it. You'll want to stay with us for ever and ever."

"I don't think our mother would like that," said Margaret, but already the music was playing, and her foot tapped along.

— *If Wishes Were Flowers* (1863),
written & illustrated by Primula
Millicent Wednesday.

Chapter 7

In Which the Kisses of Old Lovers Do Not Bear Repeating

As the magic from the broken spell dissipated into the air around them, Flavia controlled its spread, letting it pass gently among the other motes of air so that the person who wielded the spell might never know it was gone. Control was her greatest skill, after so many years alone and needing to hide her very self from so many humans.

Orlando Device, close enough to kiss, gazed into her eyes like he found her fascinating. Like *that* wouldn't cause problems, sooner or later, even if she was remotely interested in his pretty face.

Flavia coughed, and the remains of Lady Mortmain's notice-not spell in her body formed itself into a single, perfect pink rose that blossomed directly inside her mouth. She extracted it, embarrassed.

Orlando whistled. "With a talent like that, you could go on the stage," he said admiringly.

"I can think of little I would hate more than going on the stage," Flavia replied, and retreated to a less intimate distance. Orlando looked disappointed.

Rinaldo Device cleared his throat. "Good evening, Miss Wednesday," he said politely. "Is it night or day? We've lost track of everything, I'm afraid."

"Good evening works well enough," Flavia said. Her lungs felt scraped raw, but it felt comforting to know Lady Mortmain's enchantments were defeatable. "Good early hours of the dark of night isn't exactly one of the greetings they suggest in etiquette manuals." They looked rough, both of them, but oddly clean and well-fed. "Have you been here all this while?"

"I don't know what month it is," said Rinaldo, with a dry cough.

"The first week of December."

"We came here a couple of days after All Hallows. She's had us since then."

A month in chains, and they looked no worse for it. These men really were extraordinary.

Flavia turned her attention to their bonds. Rinaldo's cuffs looked like metal, but her magic did not react against them as she might expect from steel or iron. Orlando's cuffs were spiny thorn vines, but they did not feel like living plants, either.

"We can't be released by magic," Rinaldo told her. "My brother has tried to transform them, but there are so many layers of counter spell, they simply reshape themselves..."

Flavia removed her long brown gloves, tucking them both into one of the hidden pockets she had sewn into this practical day dress. Her right arm was revealed: the one made from leaves and flowers and forest, knitted into the familiar shape of an arm she had lost in the lake of the Forest of Arden.

She laid that hand on Rinaldo's bare wrist, careful not to touch his cuffs (not metal, she would smell it if it was metal, it was something much stranger). Rinaldo fell silent, his pulse jumping beneath her fingertips. She reached out to Orlando and did the same with his wrist and her ordinary, flesh-and-blood hand. She breathed again, gazing through the ordinary world to everything that lay beyond. On the other side of reality, she could see the layers of illusion placed deeply on top of each other, snagged tight like thistles twisted into stockings. She worked on peeling the illusions back, one by one, like pages in a book.

Minutes later, Flavia spat three ripe yellow plums on to the floor at their feet, and the Extraordinary and Miraculous Device Brothers found themselves to be bound by nothing but a strand of cream worsted knitting yarn.

"Wool," said Orlando, snapping it off his wrists. It broke easily. "Knitting wool? Really?"

"I imagine she used what came readily to hand," said Flavia, feeling rather pleased with himself.

Orlando leaned around and smacked the head of

his brother, who was laughing softly to himself. "You didn't know either, Professor."

"No," said Rinaldo, doubling over with laughter. "But I didn't waste a month's worth of effort trying to transform manacles that didn't exist."

Sour-face and grumbling, Orlando crossed the cellar and kicked out at the cat, which dodged him nimbly and ran behind several barrels. "Blasted shit-eating arsebucket of a mangy, flea-bitten..."

Rinaldo Device coughed. "Ladies present," he reminded his brother.

Orlando waved a hand vaguely. "I was talking to the cat."

"Yes, I rather thought you might be," Flavia said crisply. Her governess voice tended to come out in the presence of these grown men. "Never mind. You should hear what he has to say about you."

Both brothers gave her a shocked look as if she had said something that cut to the bone.

"Has... he been talking?" Rinaldo asked, snapping the yarn that twined around his own wrists.

"No," Flavia said, puzzled. "That was a joke."

Orlando pounced behind one of the barrels and came up with the yellow cat, which hissed and fizzed at him, swiping at his cheek. He held manfully on to it, keeping its claws at bay. It made a wheezing mechanical sound and spat in his face.

"Gently now, you little bastard," Orlando cooed to

it. "You've rescued us, good job and all, but we still have to rescue *you* and get you back to where you belong. Are you with us, or against us? By that I mean, do you ever want to see Buckingham Palace and your princess again?"

The cat hawked up a small object. It hit his face wetly and jangled on the floor. A copper penny, Flavia realised. Why on earth had the cat been eating bits of metal that it found, unless... "It's yours, isn't it?" she said aloud. "I mean, not your cat. But you made it, the two of you. It's an automaton."

"In a manner of speaking," said Rinaldo, heartily embarrassed. "Though the personality is not of our creation. I'd love to explain it to you, but I rather think we should be escaping before Lady Mortmain comes after us with Turkish delight and her terrifying butler."

Flavia nodded. "The kitchen was occupied when I came past. Once they go to their beds, the way should be clear to head out the back door."

"Better that than the front door," Orlando said grimly. "This might be a good time to mention, my dear Miss Wednesday, that this house has a distaste for the two of us."

"It hates our guts and would like to see them served up on a dinner plate," Rinaldo agreed. "Got the cat?"

"Got the cat," said Orlando, tucking it under one arm.

The two brothers took to the stairs with full heroic flair, ready to make their escape.

Flavia followed behind, prepared to let them behave as if they had rescued themselves, as long as they were not too insufferable about it.

~

It was hard to be heroic when your legs ached and a cat kept coughing sparks and steel fragments at you. Rinaldo was behind Orlando on the stairs, which meant that the cat under his brother's arm was pointed directly at him.

Simply by setting foot on the stairs, Rinaldo could feel the full weight of the disapproval of Number 12, Actaeon Place all over again. The sooner they got out of here, the better.

He bumped into Orlando's back at the top of the stairs. His brother floundered for a moment, trying to figure his way out of the maze of downstairs passages. Helplessly, they both turned back to Miss Wednesday, who strode past them with an implacable expression.

Rinaldo had never had a governess, but he knew an exasperated schoolteacher when he saw one. Miss Wednesday rolled her eyes at them both, and took the lead. She led them up to the kitchens, now quiet and empty. There was no sign of Lady Mortmain's cook except for a covered bowl of dough that had been left to rise. The kitchen fire was low in the grate.

"Along there," Miss Wednesday said in a calm, assured voice that made Rinaldo feel that all was right with the world. "Around the corner to the scullery, there's a door into the yard, and a gate that leads to the street behind. Be quick. Every door in the house is connected to a bell, so Mr Graves will be awoken the second you go through."

Rinaldo noted her use of 'you' and was discomfited by it. "Miss Wednesday, you *are* coming with us? You must. When Lady Mortmain discovers we are gone, she will be furious..."

"Not to mention that butler, vicious old carcass that he is," Orlando agreed. "You should take your chance to get out while you can."

Flavia shook her head. "I'm not leaving without the children. Believe me, we will be leaving, very soon. But that is our journey. Forgive me, but I don't see either of you as being of the slightest bit of help."

That stabbing feeling in Rinaldo's chest was his wounded pride, yes? He took her point, though part of him longed to argue it further. It wasn't often he got a protective urge for anyone but his brother (except Ygraine, of course, but the least said about her, the better). He was mortified that they might have endangered this strange and unusually confident young lady.

Orlando shrugged, not seeming bothered either way. Clearly he had reached his limits of chivalry. "Your funeral, miss. Come on, Professor, let's go."

Rinaldo lingered for a moment, even as Orlando headed around the corner to check the door for himself. "Are you sure? Miss Wednesday, we can't thank you enough, but —"

"Allow yourself to be rescued, for heaven's sake," she said impatiently. "You are in far graver danger from this house than I. It's rather fond of me, actually."

"If you need to find us, we'll be..."

"No, don't tell me anything." Her eyes widened with alarm. "Lady Mortmain has already taken secrets from my mind."

If he was the sort of hero who did that sort of thing, this was the point where he would sweep her off to safety. That was the storybook ending anyone might expect.

Rinaldo was not used to being rescued by anyone other than himself.

Orlando marched back to them both and seized hold of on his brother's arm with the hand he wasn't using to keep the cat steady. "Rinaldo," he said in a low growl. "We have no choice in this. We have to get out of here."

"If it wasn't for the damned cat," Rinaldo said in frustration, and reluctantly turned to follow his brother.

Ygraine would never forgive him, if they didn't sort this mess out once and for all. And Rinaldo did want to make it up to her, however impossible it seemed. Perhaps she wouldn't be quite so angry about it all, now things had died down.

He glanced back once, and saw that Miss Wednesday was smiling. "Someday you're going to have to tell me that story," she said. "I shall burn with curiosity about that awful cat of yours, until we meet again."

"It's a promise," Rinaldo said.

Miss Wednesday turned and left them to it. She didn't glance back in their direction at all.

~

Allow yourself to be rescued was easier said than done.

As soon as Miss Wednesday's presence was removed, the house started working against the Device brothers with a renewed fervour. They had not even reached the kitchen door before the tiles rocked beneath their feet and a large copper wash tub skidded out in front of them to bar their way.

"Ha," said Orlando, with a bark of laughter. "It thinks you might be intimidated by something made out of metal. How quaint."

Rinaldo flattened the tub with a gesture. He felt in control of his magic, powerful. It was good to be free of those chains, even if they had not been chains at all.

He turned his attention to the cable that ran from the door to along the edge of the ceiling. "That's the bell that alerts the butler every time a door opens."

"Excellent," said Orlando. "See to it, my good fellow."

Now they were no longer imprisoned in the dungeon, Orlando seemed happy for his brother to do all the magic again, instead of begging to borrow Rinaldo's scraps.

Rinaldo reached out to the bronze bell, putting a spark of himself into its thick inner workings, willing it to stay quiet. Meanwhile, he tore a sharp sliver from the copper washtub and levitated it like a knife to work on cutting the bell's cable. "We'll be quiet as the grave," he promised.

"Graves, you mean," said Orlando. "Glad the butler won't lose his beauty sleep." He hesitated as Rinaldo tugged open the wide, silent back door to release. "I don't like this any more than you do," he added. "Leaving our fairy governess here on her own. But I do believe Miss Wednesday can take care of herself. With her magic all stems and flowers, she's a better match for the Mortmain witch than either of us."

"We'll come back for her," Rinaldo muttered.

His brother pulled a face. "I don't want to come back here, *ever*. Even the door frame is glaring at me."

"Time to go, then. Come on!"

Together, the Extraordinary and Miraculous Device Brothers ran out into the cold night air of a London December, and into the yard of Number 12, Actaeon Place.

Free, finally, of the house.

~

F lavia stood outside the kitchen for a short
moment, to catch her breath pull herself
together. *The children.* No matter what
happened, she must be near the children when Lady
Mortmain discovered that her prisoners had disappeared into the night.

Flavia hurried along the passage to the servants'
stair, but was halted when a figure swung around the
corner and nearly bumped into her. The Honourable
Perrault Gloucester. His eyes gleamed behind the
silver spectacles he always wore. "Why, Miss Wednesday. An odd time to be out and about."

This was a night for standing too close to gentlemen, apparently. Another young lady might find it
thrilling. Flavia mostly found it tiresome.

She had been right to be wary of Perrault taking an
interest in her. His hands brushed her arms, far too
intimate to be respectable. Too late, she realised that
she had not replaced her brown silk gloves. In the dark
passage he did not seem to notice (for now) that one of
her arms was made from a braided assortment of
garden clippings. His eyes were locked on to hers, and
he swayed slightly. Was he drunk?

"Dashmond needs warm milk, sir," Flavia said, as

the first thing that came into her head. "He has night-mares." Perrault's fingers were actually stroking her grass arm, now. Digging in, past the surface. How could he not have noticed the stems and stalks?

"We all have bad dreams at times." Perrault turned her around, steering her into the kitchen as if she were a wheelbarrow. "Let me help you find that milk. I believe Mrs Brundage has retired for the night, but I know this kitchen inside out."

"Yes, I remember," said Flavia, trying to draw away from him, but his hand continued tight over her elbow as he pushed her onwards. "Sir, I really must ask you to let go of me."

She did not threaten to scream, because one did not make a threat one was not willing to follow through with. She did not wish to wake the household, not now. Those hapless Device brothers needed every second she could give them.

Perrault flattened himself against her back, no longer even pretending that he had honourable intentions. His breath was hot in her ear. "Oh, Flaxenseed. I don't think that's what you really want."

Flavia went cold inside.

Quicksilver.

She tore herself away from the warm, clammy arms of the human man — of the person she had believed to be the Honourable Perrault Gloucester. He smirked at her as she searched his face for any sign of the only

119

person in the world who called her Flaxenseed, apart from her mother.

"It's really you," she breathed. Even in that male body, so tall and angular, she could see it now she knew to look for it. The body language, the wicked twist of her mouth.

This was Quicksilver, her friend, her enemy. Beloved, once.

In the borrowed body of a human.

"At last, you see me," said the Hand of the Faerie Queen through Perrault's mouth. "I thought I would die of boredom, pretending to be this waste of flesh."

"What have you done to him?" Flavia could not remember what colour Perrault's eyes had been before the fairy lord possessed him. Blue, grey, brown? It hardly signified. They were silver now, behind the spectacles. How could she have missed that? "Is he still in there with you? Did you hollow him out completely before you climbed inside? Does Lady Mortmain know you're here?"

Quicksilver laughed merrily, not bothering to answer any questions. She came at Flavia fast and hard, shoving her against Mrs Brundage's pantry door. "You sound like a mortal," she said, hands cupping Flavia hips with an old familiarity, as if she was about to go to her knees, kiss her way upwards, all tongue and teeth. "Chatter and air."

Flavia had been trying so hard to be human, to do the right thing by the children, to deal with everything she had sacrificed when she betrayed her own mother. And here was Quicksilver, stirring everything up all over again. Anger flared inside her. "*How* are you here? If the fairies can escape like this, can climb out of their prison to steal the bodies of mortals, why haven't they done it before?"

"What makes you think we haven't?" Quicksilver laughed. "How do you think you squeezed out of our home and made your life here? You don't think you really floated here on a dandelion seed?"

Flavia stared up at her, sick inside. "Don't. Don't say that."

"Your precious mother reached out and killed a squalling newborn babe, pushed you inside it like an acorn into the earth and left you to grow there. No wonder you're as much one of them as one of us."

"Stop it!" Flavia lost control. Her illusion of humanity covering everything but her grass arm bled off her skin. She shone out green, green all over. The parsley and onions hanging from hooks near the stove burst into flower and root, growing as if they were planted in a forest. Mrs Brundage's bread dough roiled and bubbled in its bowl and grew so large that it oozed over the sides.

Her arm burst into bloom, bright pink blossoms and yellow marigolds pushing up and out of the articulating muscles and veins she had built for herself out of stems and grass.

"That's my girl," said Quicksilver inside Perrault's

body, and she kissed her, his tongue mashing hotly into Flavia's mouth.

There had been a time when Flavia welcomed Quicksilver's kisses. *How we danced.*

Flavia had never tasted the food of her mother's land in those dreams that allowed her to cross between worlds. She had never smelled the air or the trees of the island that kept Faerie in exile. But she had danced with them, her fairykin. She had tossed aside everything Great-Aunt Primula Millicent insisted upon: modesty and decorum and ladylike behaviour.

Where had that baby come from, for her mother to steal?

Was Primula Millicent my mother after all? An unwed spinster with a baby swelling inside her, and that baby made over into me, a fairy green creature with bright eyes? Is that why she hated me?

Clothes made no sense among the fairies. They valued garments only for beauty, and happily discarded them in favour of masks (their true faces) and trailing hair and dew-kissed nudity. When she dream-walked among them, Flavia — *Flaxenseed* — allowed the mortal rules to fall away like droplets of water in a river. Like a corset, unraveled and unwound so that every rounded curve of her body could be unfettered in the bright air of the isle of Faerie.

Even now, she could not stand the constraints of a corset. She knew the alternative, and it was glorious.

Quicksilver had been there in the dance, watching her with bright eyes from behind her perfect mask.

On the morning that Flavia awoke naked on the lawn of her Aunt's little cottage, she tried to hide the swollen marks of Quicksilver's kisses on her throat and breasts and mouth, but Great Aunt Primula Millicent found her out. The old lady's anger had all but set fire to the thatch, and she never looked at Flavia again without disgust and disappointment.

Flavia would not give up the dreams of Faerie, and of that wicked fairy who danced with her: her first best friend and her first love. She would not give up the possibility that someday her true mother, her *fairy* mother, might acknowledge her existence. She kept dreaming and dancing the nights away even as she slaved away in the unromantic halls of the School of Good Wives and God's Mercy.

It was not an island cut off from the mortal world, but it was still an exile.

At the age of seventeen, Flavia took her first job, with the Earnsworths of Dorchester Grove: taking on the responsibility of two young ladies who knew only a little less about the world than she did. It was her task to teach them the ways of *ladylike*, to nag them about deportment and piano lessons and mathematics. She helped them tame their minor magic into something so small and insignificant that it would not affect their chances at a successful season of husband-hunting.

By day, she wore her governess gowns, buttoned up the neck, with a prim expression to match.

At night, Flavia ran free with the faeries, naked and wild.

"I want a mask," she had begged Quicksilver one night as they sprawled side by side on a bed of bracken. She sipped from a cup of honey wine she could barely taste, and watched the green and brown limbs of her kinfolk swirl and sing around the trees in an endless pattern. "I feel naked without a true face of my own."

"Flaxenseed," Quicksilver mocked lightly, caressing her breast through the torn remains of yet another night-rail. Flavia could never think why she was always wearing the things in her dream. They never lasted for long. "You *are* naked."

"Not one of you shows your bare face," Flavia protested. "Why should I be different?"

"You are different," Quicksilver told her. "You're not really one of us."

It stung, that casual dismissal. Flavia was a fairy, not a mortal. Was her whole life not shaped around serving them all, and preparing for the day she would set them all free? She was supposed to be their champion.

Flavia had pulled away from Quicksilver's hands, that night. The honey wine slopped on the forest floor.

"What do I have to do, to be worthy of a true face? I don't belong anywhere *else*."

Quicksilver darted at her, swift as a squirrel, and pushed her on to her back. Straddling her waist with her narrow thighs, she lay fingers over Flavia's face, forming a kind of mask around her eyes. "Do you feel different now?" she challenged. "A true fairy of the greenwood?"

Flavia's breath caught in her throat, gazing through the threaded fingers at Quicksilver, feeling everything. The stickiness of the honeyed wine beneath her hip. The warmth of skin on skin. The scent of peppermint in the air. "Do I look different?" she whispered.

Quicksilver was aroused, the nipples of her small, perfect breasts peaked tightly. Her eyes flashed silver behind her true face, the mask of braided ivy. Her breath came quickly, as if she could not bear to wait seconds — one, two, three — before she kissed Flavia again.

This was love. How could it be anything else?

"You are our future," Quicksilver breathed. "You are our escape. We all know that. You are our key in the lock."

She slid her fingers deep, making a game of it.

"Well, then," said Flavia, arching with pleasure. She might not be able to taste their food or drink, but she could feel *this*. "Shouldn't you be properly grateful?"

125

"Little acorn," whispered her friend. "What makes you think we're not grateful?"

She kissed her then, a rough graze of teeth and tongue that heated Flavia all the way down to her knees. The honey wine was less than water in her mouth, but she knew the taste of Quicksilver, all apples and grass and skin. Damp and hot together, they touched and they took and they gave.

Of all the things about Faerie of which Great-Aunt Petula Millicent would not approve, this was the best and the worst.

When the two of them were sated, sticky and done with each other, Quicksilver laughed a merry laugh, licking salt off Flavia's skin — dream skin, dream pleasure, here and not-here.

"You shall have your true face, Flaxenseed," she promised. "When you have earned it."

In that moment, all Flavia wanted was for Quicksilver to know her worth.

Here in the kitchen, she tasted ashes in her mouth. Flavia stood still as Perrault's mouth ravaged hers. She jerked her head to one side, to force the kiss to end. She could do that, though her captor held both her arms in her hard grip. "Talk to me," Flavia insisted. "What have you done?"

Quicksilver laughed at her, pressing in against her with an awful intimacy in this other body. Perrault's body. "Wouldn't you like to know?"

"You're trapped here, in a body that has no magic. What's the point?"

"No magic?" Quicksilver laughed harder and longer. "My sweetling. Little acorn. Don't you know what's in this house? Haven't you realised yet? I can have anything I want." Her face — Perrault's face — twisted into a cruel smile. "I'm an Honourable Sir Muckety Muck now, and in this world of mortals that means I can have anything I want. I can beat you bloody on this floor, or rape you against that wall while you scream, and they would line up to say: yes my lord, shall we clear her away to the gutter now, my lord, do you want her taken up to your room for further savagery, my lord? *That's what humans are.*"

Flavia stared at her, barely comprehending the words. Trust Quicksilver to set one foot in the mortal world, and immediately discover how many different abuses of power there were.

Quicksilver leaned in with that vicious mouth of hers again, and Flavia braced herself to endure another unpleasant kiss. A copper pot swung out of nowhere and smashed Quicksilver in the side of the head. She slammed into the pantry door and fell lifeless to the ground. Mrs Brundage stood over the body, her face a picture of grim determination. "That is not my Lord Perry," she declared.

127

Flavia, finally released from Quicksilver's hold, could feel the bruises starting to form on the arm that was still mostly human. Even her stalks-and-leaves arm felt sorry for itself.

"No," she said, starting to shudder as her body caught up with the shock of the last few moments. "It's not him. I'm so sorry. I don't know if you're ever going to get him back."

HER FIRST DUTY, *in large establishments and where it is requisite, should be to set her dough for the breakfast rolls, provided this has not been done on the previous night, and then to engage herself with those numerous little preliminary occupations which may not inappropriately be termed laying out her duties for the day. This will bring in the breakfast hour of eight, after which, directions must be given, and preparations made for the different dinners of the household and family.*

In a magical household, our cook must be aware of the habits of her master and mistress, for if magic is worked at particular times of day or night, it can have dire consequences for the contents of the larder, or a recipe-in-progress.

Necromancy, for example, has an unfortunate effect on the setting of gelatine. Especially when it is pineapple-flavoured.

— Mrs Morrigan's Guide to Household Etiquette (1832)

Chapter 8

A Treacherous Tour Through a Hazardous House, Rife with Secrets and Surprises

The Scottish cook looked rather distressed, for someone wielding such a large and heavy copper pot. "Is he dead, lass?"

Flavia nudged the fallen Quicksilver with her foot. "He's still breathing."

She, she added silently.

"Not that one," Mrs Brundage said. "I mean my Master Perry. Is he alive in there? Or did that creature kill him to wear him like a coat?"

"I don't know," Flavia admitted.

"You're one of them," said the cook, pointing the pot at her. "One of them creatures."

Flavia shook her head quickly. "No. Of course I'm not."

"I've got eyes, lassie. You're green as a salad."

Oh, well, yes. There was that. She had forgotten how clearly she was exposed right now. Flavia concentrated for a moment, pulling the illusion back over her skin. "I can explain." She rummaged in her dress pocket for one of her brown silk gloves, and pulled it roughly over her twisted botanical arm.

"I have no doubt." There was no friendliness in Mrs Brundage's face now. "I think it's time we woke up her ladyship, don't you? She'll be wanting to deal with all this."

Flavia could not think of anything less desirable than alerting Lady Mortmain. But short of smothering Quicksilver with a pillow, she had no idea what else could be done. "If you think that's best," she agreed.

A door banged somewhere, and Mrs Brundage frowned. "Is that the back door?"

"Someone must have left it open," Flavia said. "I'll check for you."

She was not going to run away, not with the children still upstairs, but she needed some fresh air, if only for a moment. And she wanted to be sure that Rinaldo and Orlando had actually left the premises.

Before the cook could stop her, Flavia scurried off to the scullery, to where the back door had been left flapping in the night breeze. Someone had cut through the cable so that a bell was not jangling in Mr Graves' room, for which they could all be thankful.

The Brothers Device, she had to assume.

Flavia stood there for a moment, wondering if they had got away. The yard was a mess. Pots were over-turned, and the ground dug up in welts. Various tools and implements lay in a wide scatter pattern, as if there had been a fight. She saw a boot that looked a lot like Orlando's half-buried in the dirt. The gate was firmly secured, and Flavia had a feeling that it was glaring at her.

Had the house fought them every step of the way? Or had something else happened to thwart their escape? Flavia closed the door and withdrew back into the kitchens, willing herself not to wonder or care. She had done enough for the Extraordinary and Miraculous Device Brothers. She had released them from the cellar. If they were so miraculous, they could jolly well get on with rescuing themselves from now on. She had other responsibilities.

Slowly, she returned to the kitchen, ready to explain anything to Mrs Brundage that needed explaining. The cook stood poking at her exploded bread dough with disgust. That must be why she had popped back down to the kitchen before retiring for the night. If not for that bread dough, Flavia would be dead at Quicksilver's hands. "And another thing, lassie," the Scottish cook started to say.

A cry of warning flew out of Flavia's throat as Perrault rose up behind Mrs Brundage, blood matted on the side of his face. There was no copper pan within reach now, only the ceramic bowl of dough. Mrs Brundage grabbed for it, but it slipped from her fingers and smashed on the floor. She backed away from him, until she reached the cupboards.

"Do you know what the best thing is about this weak mortal body, without a spark of magic in it?" Quicksilver grated in the voice of the Honourable Perrault, who had lacked this chilly malice. "I can play with all the cold iron that I wish."

The pots in this kitchen were mostly copper or bronze and other magic-friendly alternatives. The knives, though — there were steel knives here, sealed away in a wooden block for when the cook needed something with a proper edge to it.

Flavia reached for her own magic, flinging tendrils of ivy formed from air to seize Quicksilver, pull her away from the cook.

Quicksilver spun around, holding a hilt in each hand. The ivy fell apart into motes of air again. Quicksilver smiled with Perrault's face. "It hurts," she said. "My magic can feel the iron through his body. But look. I can still hold it."

"You're not my boy," the cook spat at her. "There's nothing real about you."

"Step away," Flavia cried. "Mrs Brundage, please run."

Shaking her head, the cook seized the nearest tool that could be used as a weapon — a marble rolling pin — and advanced on Quicksilver. "Those knives are not yours," she declared. "They're mine, and I'll have them back, thank you very much."

Quicksilver stabbed Mrs Brundage in the throat,

both knives at the same time. Bright red burst from her, all over Perrault's shirt.

This was a fairy death, despite the iron in the knives. As the cook's body fell heavily to the floor, the blood pouring out of her body became a spray of scarlet petals, tumbling and whirling across the pristine tile of the floor.

Flavia would have screamed, but there was no breath in her lungs, nothing but fear and helpless rage. Nothing she could do for Mrs Brundage now.

She ran, knowing that Quicksilver would come after her next.

She skidded through the tiny walkway behind the larder. Her first instinct was to reach the lowly servants' stair at the back, because that was the way she always used if she did not have the children at her side.

But this was survival, and the back stair was too secluded. Besides, the last thing she wanted to do was to lead Quicksilver to the nursery where Queenie and Dash were sleeping.

So Flavia ran up the other kitchen stairs, the nicer ones, called the butler's stair because servants were only allowed up that way when commandeered by the butler himself to carry trays of food directly to the family.

Flavia ran upwards, flight after flight. Finally, she flung herself through the green baize floor to the family rooms on the second floor, hurrying past the elegant dining room.

She was going to have to find Lady Mortmain. Perhaps the lady of the house knew already that Quicksilver the fairy had taken over the body of her brother-in-law. If Quicksilver was her spy in the house of Tanaquil Gloriana, then Lady Mortmain might have planned for Perrault's body to be used thus.

But Flavia would never believe that Lady Mortmain would approve of Quicksilver killing Mrs Brundage, no matter what secrets she had learned. She might be a ruthless enchantress, but she had a reputation for treating her servants well.

The image of Mrs Brundage and all that blood (rose petals, torn and scattered) exploded into Flavia's mind. She could not do anything but gasp for air for several seconds. Where was she? Was Quicksilver even in pursuit, or was she up to some other nefarious deed elsewhere in this house?

Flavia could hear the pounding of her own blood in her ears. She forced herself to breathe more calmly so she could creep quietly through the maze of corridors, parlours and ante-rooms that opened up like the leaves of a cabbage on this floor, circling around the grand staircase.

It was a relief to reach the library. This at least was one of the rooms more familiar to her. From here, Flavia could navigate up into the bedrooms of the family.

This was a terrible idea. Who was she to wake the

mistress of the house? Perhaps she should try Mr Graves first.

Flavia shook herself. She had never felt more like a servant in her life, and it was not a mindset that was *helpful* right now.

The floor creaked, elsewhere on this floor. Flavia froze, and heard a muffled thump, then a mutter in a low male voice. She slipped into the library and hid herself among the shelves.

More creaking. Someone was here in the room with her. She felt their presence, warm and human. Was that magic she sensed? She was too shattered to rally the concentration needed to recognise whose magic, or even what kind of magic it might be. She shuffled back, further and further, until she was in the tightest corner, surrounded by large atlases and volumes of rural poetry.

There was a crash, and another mutter, and this one had the words 'damned cat' in it. Flavia stood up and march back around the shelves to peer accusingly into the shadows. "Rinaldo Device?" she whispered. "Is that you?"

"Miss Wednesday!" the shadow before her declared, sounding relieved. Also, loud.

"Shhhh!" She seized his sleeve and dragged him back into the corner of the library with her. It was certainly Rinaldo, in a worse state than when he left the house by the back door. His trousers were ripped, his hair mussed wildly, and his shirt had some kind of black tar on it. She refused to be pleased to see him, just because it meant she wasn't alone any more. "You're supposed to be gone," she whispered, her hands curling into his shirt. "And safe. With your stupid cat."

"The house had other ideas," Rinaldo whispered back. "I don't know the enchantress has done it deliberately, or if it's just the way her magic works, this place *hates* us. The front steps tried to eat Orlando when we arrived, and the carpet has definite opinions about whether we should be here at all. We got as far as the yard, but it attacked us."

"The yard attacked you," Flavia repeated, remembering the mess she had seen out there. "Or the house?"

"Bit of both, really," Rinaldo said, sounding awfully embarrassed. "There was this tree by the gate that wouldn't let us leave, and then the bloody cat ran off down the coal chute and when we tried to follow it sort of swallowed up Orlando, and I had to fight my way through the..."

Flavia hugged him. She had not meant to, not in the least, but she could not take his chatter any longer. Her gloved arms hooked around the his neck so as to cling to him more effectively.

For a precious moment she allowed herself to take comfort in the presence of another person of whom she was not the least bit afraid.

Rinaldo smelled of dust and the not-quite-lemon

scent of memory charms. Honestly, that was better than she could have hoped for in a man who had been chained in a cellar for more than a month.

"Uh," Rinaldo murmured, as she continued to cling. "This is awkward. I hope I haven't given you any reason to have any sort of romantic expectations. You're very nice. Nothing against you. It's not my... oh hell, are you crying?"

Flavia sobbed quietly into his shoulder. "I'll stop in a minute," she promised, heaving against his chest.

"Not to worry," Rinaldo said, sounding really quite worried indeed. He patted her on the back, in an extremely awkward manner. It helped more than one might expect.

Once she could bear it, Flavia pulled away, removed an embroidered handkerchief from her own pocket, and blew her nose. It was one of the hankies that Queenie had done up for her, before All Hallows, when they were still on friendly terms. Forget-me-nots and test tubes were messily embroidered along the edges, along with a list of ingredients required to brew a basic headache tea.

"Are you all right?" Rinaldo asked, still sounding rather wary.

"There is a murderer in this house, a fairy called Quicksilver, who has commandeered the body of the Earl's younger son, the Honourable Perrault Gloucester," Flavia replied, sniffling a bit into the handkerchief.

"Oh dear."

"Indeed."

"That's not good, I expect."

"And I wouldn't worry yourself about romantic intentions," she added. "I prefer the company of ladies, on the whole. Though my taste in ladies is questionable at best."

Rinaldo made a small, strangled sound at her honesty, and then blurted: "I prefer to be clear of the whole business."

"That's all right, then."

"Yes."

They both stared at each other, a little shocked at having been so... well. Intimate, Flavia thought, was probably the word.

"We have to warn Lady Mortmain," she added. "Right now."

"She'll lock me in the cellar again," Rinaldo moaned.

"Perhaps," Flavia said impatiently. "And I'll rescue you again. It's hardly relevant. Everyone in this house is in the most terrible danger."

Mostly me. And you, if she finds us together.

"Also, you have to find her first," Rinaldo added. "The lady's not in her bedroom."

Flavia blinked twice. "How do you know that?"

"When I got separated from my brother, I thought about the worst place he could possibly have ended up in this house, and I checked there first." Rinaldo gave her a weak smile. "My brother is also, uh. Has a questionable taste in ladies, one might say."

Flavia chose not to ask further questions. "If she is not in her bed, then where can we find her?" They must move soon, must do something, or she was going to start crying again, and this time she might not stop. Mrs Brundage had been *lovely*.

She knew she was being wet. Miss Troughton, her old games mistress, would be thoroughly disgusted with her. Nevertheless, all she wanted to do was curl up in a bathtub and weep.

"There's," said Rinaldo, and then stopped, tilting his head as if listening to something that Flavia could not hear. "There's a lot more metal in this house than there used to be," he said in dawning realisation. "Can you feel that?"

Flavia shuddered, remembering the gleam of cold iron in the kitchen knives. "Is there?" One of the things she had liked most about this house was that most of the metal of the kind that distressed her was outside the walls, in the city beyond.

"Bronze, mostly," Rinaldo breathed. "Upstairs, above our heads. I can *feel* it. Good bronze. Warm. The kind I used to work with at the palace. It wasn't here when Orlando and I first arrived in this house. It's new."

"Will it make your magic stronger, if we get you near it?" Flavia asked. "If Quicksilver is still carrying iron, my magic won't be able to do much against her. I've too much greenwood in my blood."

Her thoughts flitted to Quicksilver's taunt, that there must have been a baby whose life was stolen to make Flavia real. If that was true, how was it that Quicksilver could hold cold iron in the body of Perrault, while Flavia had never been able to touch the stuff?

"I believe so," said Rinaldo thoughtfully. "Are you saying it's my turn to be the shining knight?" he added, finding some humour in the situation.

"It's only fair," agreed Flavia. "You are named for one, after all."

~

R inaldo was not feeling particularly heroic. Theirs had been the world's worst escape. He was still bruised all over from fighting with the backyard of Number 12 Actaeon Place, and he had lost track of both his brother and the yellow cat that started all this.

The house hated him so much, and yet... that bronze. It called to him, sparking against his magic. A siren song of power and sympathy.

Even without Miss Wednesday's assent, he would have gone after the bronze. He did not think that he could stay away, not with the metal calling to him from above his head.

Several flights of stairs later, it remained above his head.

"This is the top floor," Miss Wednesday whispered to him. They were holding hands out of sheer practicality as they navigated the stairs in the dark.

The house liked her as much as it hated him. It was only her close proximity that had allowed him to use these stairs at all. As it was, the banister leaned away from Rinaldo so that he could not use it, and at least three mysterious trapdoors had broken through the carpet between here and the library in the hopes of catching him unaware.

"What's above us?" he asked her.

"Only the attic. It's a sort of portrait gallery, otherwise completely empty. They use it to travel between here and Gloucester Worth."

"Saves on train fare, I expect." There was a silence from Miss Wednesday. Rinaldo could all but hear the cogs in her mind turning. "What?"

"I was just thinking," she murmured. "A house this big has space for a larger attic than the one I saw when I first arrived. Several attics, in fact. Perhaps I didn't see as much as I thought I did."

The bronze was tugging at Rinaldo, calling him up. "Let's go."

Flavia did not move. "The nursery is on this floor. I must check on the children. Quicksilver knows what they mean to me."

Rinaldo could not argue with that, not with a mad

knife-wielding fairy loose in the house. "Makes sense. Children, then attics."

Flavia led the way to the nursery, and stopped to light a candlestick just inside the doorway. Rinaldo heard her gasp as she raised the light.

The girl, Miss Queenie Gloucester, was fast asleep in a narrow bed near the window. The other bed, the one belonging to the scamp called Dash, was empty. Flavia made a small keening noise, and Rinaldo took her hand again, squeezing it firmly in his own. "He could be anywhere," he assured her. "Boys do that sort of thing. Maybe he's curled up with my cat somewhere. Kindred souls, those two, trouble on legs."

Or three, perhaps. 'Trouble on legs' was as apt a description of Orlando as Rinaldo had ever made before.

Flavia nodded. "I should never have left them," she muttered.

"What about the girl?"

"I'd better wake her up."

Queenie Gloucester awoke slowly. "What's happening?" she asked, rubbing sleep out of her eyes. Then, in a sharper tone once she realised who had awoken her: "What have you done now?"

"Your brother is missing," Flavia told her. "Do you think your aunt might have taken him?"

"I don't know," said Queenie. She glanced up, and directly at Rinaldo. "Hello, Mr Device. It's a little early for winter solstice, isn't it?"

"Just a flying visit, Miss Gloucester," said Rinaldo with a short bow. "Do you happen know what occupies the attic of this house? Something large and bronze?"

Queenie gave him a searching look, then tugged on the drawer to her bedside table. "I have some lozenges you two should probably eat before we go. The last thing we need is you falling under my aunt's enchantments."

Rinaldo stared in awe at the jar of small sugary beads she produced. "Those sweeties counter Lady Mortmain's enchantments?"

"Oh yes," said Queenie.

"Can I fill my pockets?"

~

Queenie Gloucester, still in her night-rail with a stout woollen robe over the top, clutched a small lantern she claimed to be both 'everlasting' and her own invention and *much better than candles, Miss Wednesday, are you even living in the eighteenth century?* She led Flavia and Rinaldo back down one floor, despite their protests. "There are two attics," she informed them. "And you can't get from one to the other. It's complicated, to reach the secret one. We're going to need help."

Rinaldo glanced at Flavia, wondering if they should share the information about the girl's fairy-possessed and quite murderous Uncle Perrault, but she caught the question in his eyes and shook her head firmly. All right, then.

"When you say help..." Flavia began to say, but Queenie was ahead of her, knocking on one of the bedroom doors.

"Grandfather?" she asked, and pushed the door open when she heard a murmur from within. "I'm awfully sorry. But things have taken a serious turn. I think Aunt Elspeth might have moved into your old workshop."

This bedroom was the first room in the house that did not have some kind of botanical pattern of wallpaper. It was striped, instead, grey and white. An austerity reflected in the simple furnishings, apart from an enormous four poster bed that looked as if it belonged in a museum.

An elderly man in a cotton nightcap sat up in bed. He regarded the small party on his threshold with a stern, glittering gaze. "You'd better come in, and close the door behind you," said the Earl of Shuttlesworth.

Flavia appeared lost for words. This was highly out of character based on the little time Rinaldo had known her. They went in together, though the carpet edging of the bedroom did its best to prevent him getting over the threshold. He had to be quick to avoid the door banging back in his face of its own volition.

"Surprised to see him?" he whispered to Flavia as Queenie hugged her grandfather.

"Honestly? I though he was dead and they were hushing it up for some reason," she whispered back, only to look embarrassed when the Earl turned his piercing expression upon her. "I am so sorry to disturb your rest, my lord," she added.

"I'm an old man, sleep has little interest for me," he declared in reply. "Now then, my Queenie. What's this about the workshop? I closed it up, you know. Retired. Heartbreaking business, alchemy. I tried for forty years to reproduce my father's secret formula, and what do I have to show for it? Bunions, a nagging cough, and these creaking bones." He gave a hard look at Rinaldo, who shifted uncomfortably under his gaze. "Do I know you, young man?"

Rinaldo could not say for sure. His life at the palace had meant a great deal of scrutiny from old white men: the Britannian lords of the land, patrons and purveyors of magic. This Earl could had been in attendance at any of the formal dinners where the Queen chose to show off her Miraculous and Extraordinary Device Brothers and their uncanny tricks. It all blurred, after a while.

"That's Mr Rinaldo Device," said Queenie. "He used to be one of her Majesty's Royal Engineers, but Aunt Elspeth has had him locked up in the cellar for the last month. He believes my aunt might have been building something terrible in your workshop. Something made of metal."

"I didn't say that, my lord," Rinaldo protested, but

Queenie's words resonated within him. "Though it may be true."

Queenie gave him a scornful look, as if he was a fool not to have thought of why there might be a large quantity of bronze in the attic of this house.

Rinaldo's hands felt warm for a moment, as if he was working in metal. Something surged through his mind — not quite a recollection, but a shadow of a thought he could not quite grasp. "Lady Mortmain has been using memory charms," he said, flexing and stretching his hands. "On the servants, on me and my brother. I rather think — if she has brought in a large quantity of bronze, chances are it was for me. For me to make something for her with my magic."

All those gaps in their memory, he and Orlando, chained up in the cellar. Was this where he had been?

"There's also a knife-wielding fairy loose in the house," added Flavia.

Queenie tsked. "And when were you going to mention *that*?"

"I'm sorry." Clearly, Flavia had hit the limit of how many secrets she could keep. "He has taken over the form of your younger son," she said to the Earl. "I saw Perrault kill Mrs Brundage in her kitchen when she tried to expose him as a changeling."

Queenie pressed her hands to her mouth.

The Earl threw back his covers and stood up, displaying a billowing white nightshirt that covered him majestically from neck to ankle. "Zounds, that's bad news. Can't get a reputation for letting cooks get murdered. Good ones are so hard to replace. Come, now. Let us investigate what liberties that wretched Mortmain woman has taken in my house."

The Earl marched with purpose into what looked like his dressing room. Rinaldo expected him to march right out again. Was an Earl capable of clothing himself without the assistance of an army of valets?

A moment later, Rinaldo heard a chiming sound, and a whirr that most definitely did not belong in a dressing room.

"Come along if you're coming, youngsters!" the Earl called from within.

Queenie's expression had gone from scornful all the way up to scorching. "If this violent fairy has done anything to harm Dash, Miss Wednesday. You and I are *done*."

LADY M - TRAGIC BRIDE OR BLACK WIDOW?

Eight months after the wedding of a certain Miss C (now Lady M), a funeral has been announced, and the new bride is wearing mourning dress all around town. This column should not like to throw stones, but didn't we predict a mysterious death or two once the wedding season ended?

No one would dare accuse Lady M of impropriety: her calling card is found in all the best drawing rooms, and she is known for hosting the most splendid of soirees.

What's a little murder, when one has the chance to rub elbows with the best dressed witch in Britannia?

— A London Gossip, *The Spark and Philtre Gazette*, 1863

Chapter 9

A Study in Bronze

Rinaldo had never before seen the like of the Earl of Shuttlesworth's mechanical dressing room. He was instantly in love with it. It drew them startlingly upwards with all manner of pleasing whirs and hums.

This part of the house, at least, did not wish Rinaldo ill. He in turn could happily have stayed within this copper-walled box for months, though it might be rather less comfortable once he had entirely disassembled it to see how it worked.

"As you can see, I did not entirely waste these last forty years on scientific impossibilities," said the Earl with a certain degree of pride. "If I have any regrets, it's that I bothered with the blasted philtres in the first place. I could have had one of these marvellous contraptions in every household in Britannia and then we'd have our family fortune secured, wouldn't we, my dear? The Gloucestervator!" He tapped Queenie on the chin. "Like a dumbwaiter, you see, but mechanised and far more convenient for personal travel."

"It's very clever, Grandfather," Queenie said politely. "But I find philtre-brewing a perfectly satisfying pursuit."

"Ah, well, my dear, to each his own."

"Can it move sideways as well as upwards?" Rinaldo burst out. "How does it work? Is it on cables, or are they more like vertical train tracks?"

An unlit lamp on the wall behind him burst alight, and leaned ominously in Rinaldo's direction, scorching his collar. He stepped quickly into the middle of the Gloucestervator, out of reach. So this part of the house was not entirely different.

"Stop that," the Earl said impatiently to the wall, and blew on the lamp until it quietened down.

"Your house has somewhat homicidal intentions towards me, my lord," said Rinaldo. He did not know why there was such an apologetic tone in his voice, but it seemed politic.

"So I see," said the Earl. "I shouldn't take it personally, young man. Number 12 is a temperamental sort of place, and she chooses her favourites. But she's been good to me and my family over the years."

There was a loud ding and a shudder as the dressing room arrived at their destination.

Rinaldo stepped closer to Flavia, wondering if it would be inappropriate to hold her hand again. It might be his best chance of surviving this attic, but she was lost in her own thoughts, and he did not wish to bother her.

"You're all right with bronze, aren't you?" he asked in a low voice. "It's only iron, uh, that you…"

"Bronze is fine," she said, darting a quick look at the Earl to check whether he was listening.

"Good," said Rinaldo. "Because there's a great deal of it beyond these doors. I'm a little astonished that the floorboards can support it."

The Earl painstakingly turned a long crank, levering open the doors of the Gloucestervator.

Rinaldo would have been keen to converse further with the Earl. He and Orlando had until recently been working upon a plan to install rudimentary automated doors in Buckingham Palace. Sadly, there was a time and a place for scientific discovery, and this was not it.

What Rinaldo saw beyond the doors was so incredible that he could barely fit it into his field of vision, let alone his mind.

The Gloucestervator would have to wait.

"It's beautiful," gasped Flavia.

"Diabolical," muttered the Earl of Shuttlesworth.

"So that's what she was doing all this time," declared Queenie, triumphant as if she had guessed it all along.

If this attic room had ever been a workshop, then Rinaldo was going to have to take their word for it, because all he could see was *fountain*.

It was bronze: a massive weight of bronze, shaped in a pleasing arrangement from both an aesthetic and a practical perspective. (Except of course, that if Rinaldo had been asked where to build such a thing, he would have suggested an outdoor courtyard or park, not the top floor of a London townhouse.)

Rinaldo knew his own work when he saw it. His and Orlando's. It glowed with their magical signature. How had the enchantress done that? Orlando had not been able to use his own magic for months, not after what she had done to him. He could borrow scraps from Rinaldo, perform a few basic charms, but nothing with any weight to it. Even before that, Orlando's magic had been... erratic in recent years.

No one could have built this beauty but Rinaldo and his brother at the peak of their powers. It killed him that he could not remember doing it. Somehow, in all those lost hours taken from he and his brother with the enchantress' memory charms, they had accomplished a masterpiece.

The fountain was a replica of the house in which they stood. No wonder Rinaldo had been able to navigate around Number 12 in the dark even before the assistance of Miss Wednesday. A part of him must have remembered the arrangement of rooms, however deep inside his mind it had been buried.

What stood before them, eight feet tall, was a highly detailed bronze simulacrum of Number 12, Actaeon Place, complete with tiny bronze maids and butlers and ladies and gentlemen: clockwork figures with little keys in their backs to make them work. The bronze townhouse hummed to Rinaldo, welcoming him closer. He itched to get his hands all over it, to press his sparks into its workings and draw out its history, and all its secrets.

This house, at least, would never hate him.

"What is it for?" asked Flavia behind him, sounding baffled.

Rinaldo almost snapped at her. Would anyone ask the purpose of Michelangelo's *David*? Or the *Mona Lisa*? He stepped closer, pressing his hands against the warm bronze. It welcomed him home with a hum.

"Don't touch it," Flavia warned.

"It's quite safe. It's wonderful." Rinaldo patted it lovingly. "It's mine. I made this."

"Well, obviously," she said briskly. "I recognise the style. I thought the tree at Crystal Palace was rather wonderful, and it tried to strangle me. What is it *for*, Rinaldo?"

Rinaldo hungered to impress her. This was the greatest thing he and Orlando had ever made together. Surely, she would love it once he showed her how clever it was. He circled around behind the marvel. "There are levers here and here," he said, hands sliding over the metal. "And — like this!"

The replica of Number 12 Actaeon Place burst into life, revealing the truth of its function.

"Oh!" said Queenie, with a choked gasp. "It's for *philtres*."

Rinaldo grinned stupidly, circling around the miraculous object. "Why, yes!" he exclaimed, waving his arms like the showman he had been, before his life fell apart.

Years and years of performing spectacles and miracles to starchy diplomats and disapproving ladies, at the behest of Queen Isolda. Rinaldo had the act down to a fine art, even if Orlando had always been better at the public speaking.

This particular exhibit was worth the flourish.

Water sprang up from each miniature room, channeled back and forth in all manner of calculated spouts and sprays and trickles. The water danced down chutes and up funnels. As the water played out its merry procession, the bronze townhouse came alive. The clockwork figures moved, some circling on the spot and others actually walking from room to room, performing complex rituals in a looping pattern, round and round. Rinaldo could feel how the fountain worked, every piece of it.

He could even see the patterns of the wallpaper in every room. Ivy. Pomegranate-and-cress. Marigolds in the kitchen. Clover and cornflowers in the cellar.

"We did this," Rinaldo breathed. "We made this perfect thing."

He and Orlando had been building marvels together since they were children. From figures made

155

out of hairpins and crockery, to magnificent jewelled centrepieces for the Queen's table and automated maids and footmen who responded to her every command. This was better. This was a work greater than anything they had ever done before, and Rinaldo desperately wanted to share it with his brother.

Where are you, Orlando?

Flavia did not look impressed. Standing there with the Earl of Shuttlesworth and young Queenie, her arms crossed across her sturdy bust, she was a portrait of grave suspicion.

"What's wrong?" Rinaldo asked, pushing down the sting of hurt. Dangers were abroad in this house, of course. A murderer, and suchlike. He knew that. But surely such distractions should not stop her admiring the masterwork he had created.

"Apart from the fact that Lady Mortmain took you and your brother prisoner, forced you to make this monstrosity, and wiped your memories repeatedly?" Flavia replied in a crisp voice. "Forgive me, *Mr Device*, but I find myself to be wary of magical fountains. Every chivalric romance I've ever read has made it clear that they are not to be trifled with."

The Earl perambulated around the attic room, tutting at the magical bronze fountain from every angle. "An ingenious piece of engineering and metal-lurmagic," he said finally, clapping Rinaldo on the shoulder as he passed him. "But I agree with the governess. If Elspeth Mortmain commissioned this object, then no good can come of it."

Flavia peered into the fountain, and drew in a shaky breath. "Rinaldo," she said. He could not help but wonder when it was they had dropped all pretence of formality between them. When exactly they became Flavia and Rinaldo, not Miss Wednesday and Mr Device. "Come and look at this."

Rinaldo went to her side, hoping she had found something that would allow her to see this creation of his as a wonder rather than a terror. "What is it?"

She pointed to the bronze kitchen, which flooded with water from one arcing spout of water, only to have it drain away by another chute, leaving every pot and tabletop gleaming and wet. "Do you remember making that?"

Rinaldo stared. One of the bronze figures had fallen, though it did not look like an accident so much as part of the overall design. The little doll-like cook lay sprawled on the buttercup-patterned floor tiles of her kitchen. "I must have done," he said slowly.

"You did that to her? You positioned her as dead on the floor?" Her voice was shaking.

Rinaldo's eyes travelled up across the rooms. "The others aren't as in life. Look at them, they perform a daily routine. If they reflected what was happening now, then most of them would be in bed."

"And yet, Mrs Brundage is dead in her kitchen."

"I don't know. I don't remember doing that." His

head was starting to hurt. "Are you saying I caused her murder?"

"No," said Flavia. "I'm not saying that at all." Her eyes roamed from room to room, examining each configuration. "But I would very much like to know in which room you placed the bronze doll of the Honourable Perrault Gloucester."

"I think," said a throaty, female voice. "You will probably find him in the attic."

Lady Elspeth Mortmain, golden and unruffled in an elaborate gown of widow's black and a discreetly tailored leather apron, stood in front of a door in the attic roof that had not been there before. Beside her stood an tidy gentleman in spectacles. Rinaldo guessed from the look of horror on Flavia's face that this must be her Honourable Perrault, now providing house space for Quicksilver the Fairy.

"Ah, Elspeth," said the Earl briskly. "Perhaps you can explain a few things, young lady. Last I looked, this was *my* workshop, and here you are filling it up with enormous bronze gee-gaws. I'm not convinced that it's quite the thing, don't you know. Or structurally sound, come to that."

Lady Mortmain smiled like a snake. Was she the reason Rinaldo hadn't seen his brother for hours? "With the greatest of respect, Earl," said the enchantress. "The last time you took an interest in this workshop was nearly a decade ago. It was lying neglected, and so I put it to good use."

The elderly Earl sniffed, dismissing the bronze fountain with a wave of his hand that made Rinaldo want to punch him. "I'm sure you've been productive with your time, my dear. A gentlewoman needs a hobby when she is without a husband. I'm more concerned with the fact that you appear to have done some damage to one of my sons." He looked at Perrault with a searching frown.

Perrault's face broke into an unnatural smile. "I've never felt better, father dear."

The Earl was unimpressed. "Don't speak to me, creature. I may have been a distant papa, once it became clear that neither of my sons had inherited my intellect. But that doesn't give you the right to come waltzing in and climb inside my boy as if he was a spare attic." He gave an especially stern look to Lady Mortmain. "You know this sprite murdered our cook?"

"I've already reprimanded her for that, your grace," said Lady Mortmain sweetly. "The domestic sphere is my domain. If a servant is to be killed, I prefer to handle the matter personally. Lady Quicksilver will not trespass again."

"Where's Dash?" asked Queenie Gloucester in a defiant voice. Everyone stared at the girl. She lifted her chin. "You're all being very clever and civilised, pretending this is a garden party instead of a battle. But I want to know where my little brother is, if it's all the same to you. He isn't in his bed."

Lady Mortmain's smile was so bright and so false

that she almost had a beam of light shining out from between her teeth. "Why don't you ask your governess? So meek and mild, you wouldn't think Miss Wednesday had so many secrets roiling around in that moss-green skin of hers. Perhaps that traitor sold Dashmond off to the Queen of Faerie in exchange for an acorn, or whatever the greenwood creatures use as currency."

The Perrault-Fairy gave her a leering look. "Mostly we exchange favours," she said.

Queenie stepped closer to Flavia. "Miss Wednesday's not very good at keeping secrets, actually," she said, chin high. "Or at traitoring."

"Betrayal, dear," Flavia corrected in a murmur.

"I trust her, Aunt Elspeth, and I don't trust you. What exactly is your plan for this monstrosity of a fountain?"

Lady Mortmain inhaled. Rinaldo had never really understood why Orlando was so regularly transfixed by her beauty. The proximity of the bronze fountain, however had him more unbalanced than a whole tray of enchanted Turkish delight. In this moment, the confidence of Lady Mortmain was dazzling.

She was gazing at him. Rinaldo was not used to having the enchantress look twice at him — she'd always paid far more attention to Orlando, the brother she could actually manipulate.

"Why don't you ask the man who built it?" Lady

Mortmain said with a sensuous smile. And then, they were all looking at Rinaldo.

"I don't remember," he protested. "Your memory charms. You made me forget."

"Come, my boy, you can do better than that," said the Earl. "Show a little backbone."

"Gumption," murmured Flavia.

Rinaldo reached out and brushed his hand against the warm bronze wall of the replica of the house that hated him. "When we were in the Forest of Arden," he said quietly. "Orlando and I gathered vials of water from each of the fountains. For her Ladyship."

The Earl drew in a breath. "You opened the gate to the Arden?"

"No, sir, I did that," admitted Flavia. "But Lady Mortmain had a spy in my mother's house, and she knew I had been sent to open the gate. She sent the Device brothers through on the same evening."

"Vials of water?" Queenie demanded. "You mean – philtre samples from the fountains of love and hate and youth and all that?" She pointed shakily at the new bronze fountain. "Are they all in there? My grandfather's philtre, the love-me-not, is that in there too? *Mixed together?*"

It was that last part she seemed to find most horrifying, and rightfully so.

Rinaldo gazed at the fountain, past the bronze surface and the exquisite artistry of the sculpture. There was a hive of activity within – of sparks and cogs and wheels, all humming with magic. Queenie's guess was not quite correct. The separation of the philtres had been taken into account. The fountain ran several different circuits so that different quantities of water were kept distinct from each other as they danced from room to room. "You would have needed more than what was in the vials," he muttered, lost in engineering thoughts.

"You mean you didn't know?" Lady Mortmain laughed. "The fountains of the Forest of Arden are powerful, and the waters within them contain some of the strongest magic ever known. Add one drop to any quantity of our water, and the qualities of that magic run pure. This fountain does not merely house the samples you and your brother so readily brought me — it produces more of each."

Queenie was outraged. "But that's not scientific!" she howled.

Rinaldo sympathised with her. Magic was deeply infuriating, especially when you expected it to follow certain rules and it laughed in your face.

"I've heard enough," said the Earl of Shuttlesworth in a grumpy voice. "I'm closing you down, Elspeth. We took you into our household for Carolinge's sake, after the death of that husband of yours, and I can't say it wasn't useful having a lady about the house to deal with the servants and other domestic nonsense. But now you've endangered my family. This contraption of yours is likely to drag the Gloucester name through ignominy and ill repute. It's time for you to leave my home and start behaving like a respectable widow. Elsewhere."

Lady Mortmain gave him a polite bob of her head. "You sweet old thing," she said in a voice that dripped butter and honey. "How commanding you are. It's almost endearing. But do you really think this is the first time that we have had this conversation?"

"No!" Rinaldo shouted, stepping forward too late to stop her. Lady Mortmain flicked a spark of green magic at the Earl. He stood rigid, his face falling slack.

"Now," said the enchantress in ringing tones. "Go to bed, old man. Sleep for a week. If anyone asks you to wake and eat, you may take in a little gruel to keep you going, but nothing too adventurous. We must take care of you, mustn't we? You will remember nothing about tonight. You never do."

Slowly, his slippered feet shuffling on the floor and his nightcap drooping, the Earl walked back to the Gloustercator. He looked a shadow of himself. The mechanisms started up with a whir, returning him to his room.

"You didn't have to do that," Queenie said fiercely.

"On the contrary," said Lady Mortmain, rolling her eyes . "I have to do this sort of thing *constantly*. The last thing I need is some fading patriarch deciding he has power over where I live and what I do."

"It's his house!" Queenie shouted. "He's the Earl of Shuttlesworth. You're nothing, you're just my mother's widowed sister who had nowhere else to go. They took *pity* on you."

Rinaldo leaned in to Flavia, whispering. "If you get a chance, get hold of Queenie and run like hell."

"What will you do?" Flavia replied, her lips barely moving.

"Something heroic, I expect. Draw their attention, that sort of thing. When I do it, fast as you can, get out of this house."

"We have nowhere to go. Where would be safe?"

"Buckingham Palace." The one place he had been running from all these months. Rinaldo wanted nothing more than to be back there, on his knees, confessing everything to Queen Isolda and willingly accepting any punishment she and the princess wished to bestow upon him.

Ygraine, I'm so sorry.

Flavia did not look convinced. "This is hardly the time for levity."

"I know people there," he insisted

"Well, I don't know anyone, so you'd better escape with us," she said tartly.

Rinaldo looked over to where Queenie stood arguing with her aunt. "You have to get her away from this bloody house."

"I know," Flavia whispered. "But how about if *I* draw their attention and *you* rescue Queenie, then run like hell to Buckingham Palace. Since you know so many people there."

Rinaldo saw her point, thought he hated it. "Let's make it up as we go along," he said reluctantly.

Showmanship. It had never come easily to him, but he had learned a thing or two from working with Orlando all these years. Making a fuss and a flap, putting on a spectacle of whatever you were doing, was sometimes the only way to get anything done.

You couldn't think about the consequences. That was the trick of a good performance.

Queenie was far too near her aunt to be cleanly extracted from this scene, and Rinaldo did not like the gleam in the eye of the fairy controlling Perrault Gloucester's body. Something had to be done. Something loud and brash and distracting, to allow the ladies to make their escape. Or something quiet and sneaky to get the Gloucester girl out of here while Flavia played the hero. It was a tough call.

What would Orlando do?

In a battle, it is generally agreed
    That winning is good, whether it be through
skill
        Or dumb luck. And it's preferable to bleed
        As little as possible.

— Ludovico Ariosto, *Orlando Furioso*

Chapter 10

The Water of Worlds

Flavia could not take her eyes off the roiling, churning philtres that danced from room to room in this grotesque bronze fountain. All the waters of the Forest of Arden were in there? Love, love-me-not, hate, truth, life, wisdom, know-not, oblivion, youth, transformation, undoing and the water of worlds. So much power splashing around in there. So much that could be misused.

The water of worlds.

Flavia had spent years creeping around, being polite and genteel, mimicking everything safe and sensible about Britannian society. She had been good at playing the quiet, perfect governess — too good. Even now, in the midst of such an important confrontation, every instinct was telling her to be polite.

Manners would not help now. Impertinence might.

"What are you planning to do with these philtres?" she asked aloud, interrupting the angry exchange between Queenie and her aunt.

"Isn't it obvious?" said Lady Mortmain. "I'm going to rule the Empire. Time to bring that Eirish bitch's dynasty of doomed daughters to an end. Queen Elspeth the First sounds right to me." She spread her hands wide, and a crown of flowers burst forth from her hair, with tall grass fronds spiking upwards.

Flavia smiled with an edge of pity to it. "I wasn't talking to you."

"Darling," said Quicksilver in the stuffy Upstairs voice of the Honourable Perrault. "I knew you loved me best."

Flavia ignored that. "I'm not a fool, Quicksilver. You've served my mother for a century, I'm not going to readily believe that you traded in all that power and privilege and *loyalty* for a chance to play house with a social-climbing harpy."

A shocked keening noise came from Lady Mortmain. She must be unaccustomed to rudeness from the help. It was enough to make Flavia want to think up more elaborate insults, but she could not afford to be distracted.

"So what was the plan?" she asked, still addressing Quicksilver. "You and Tanaquil Gloriana can't leave the Isle of Faerie – you couldn't even get beyond the lake. Good Queen Bess demanded that access to the

Forest of Arden was closed to humans as well as fairies. Why should she need to make such a provision? Unless there was something in Arden that could be used to release you from the exile... say, the water of worlds?"

There was a flicker in Quicksilver expression. She had guessed right.

Flavia shook her head. "You did this all wrong, Quicksilver. If you'd kept this charade going for another few weeks, you could have walked into the Forest of Arden on the winter solstice with a Gloucester child holding each hand. They would have gone *willingly* if they thought you were their trusted Uncle Perrault. Queenie would have been easily convinced it was her idea. But you couldn't bother to pantomime human for a moment longer. You had to use your brand new body to murder a sweet woman, and play a detestable cat-and-mouse game with me."

"You don't think my plan was effective?" said Quicksilver with an arched eyebrow. "I am here and the water of worlds is right before us in that pretty bronze fountain. You stand before me, Flaxenseed, to witness my success. I only need present one Gloucester child to my Queen for her ritual, and you brought one right to my feet."

Queenie trembled with a rage of her own. "You don't have my brother after all, then," she said bravely. "I'm pleased to hear it."

Apparently Flavia had a cruel streak in her after all. She was *enjoying* the expression on Lady Mortmain's face as the enchantress realised that her pet fairy spy had been serving her true queen all along. "She's not just a child," Flavia said now. "Miss Petronella Gloucester is one of the most dedicated alchemists in London. I also brought a Royal Engineer to witness your glory. Say hello to Mr Rinaldo Device, metallurmage. He's just as good at breaking machines down as he is at building them, you know."

Rinaldo, behind her, gave a small groan. "Really? That's your plan?"

"You can build another masterpiece tomorrow," Flavia insisted. "It will be even better because you'll remember doing it."

"You make a sharp point, Miss Wednesday." Rinaldo sighed, and obligingly raised his arms. Sparks flew off his skin as he whirled his hands around like he was a symphony conductor.

"No!" screamed Lady Mortmain. Her magic burst out of her in a cloud of spring blossom and perfumed pollen, directed at the three of them: Flavia, Rinaldo and Queenie. Flavia felt it roll over their heads and hit the back wall of the attic before dispersing.

This particular expression on Lady Mortmain's face was even more enjoyable.

"Lozenges," breathed Queenie. "Her magic can't touch us."

"The aniseed's a little strong," Flavia agreed. She still had the morsel of sweet under her tongue, dissolving slowly. "But on the whole, it was a worthy investment of your time. You might want to consider applying for the patent."

Bronze heaved and creaked and sighed as Rinaldo Device tore at the magic within the sinister copy of Number 12, Actaeon Place. A bronze wall peeled away, and hit the attic floor with a thumb. Water sprayed out of the side of the fountain, in several different jets.

"Most dedicated alchemist in London," muttered Queenie, as if the words gave her power. She worked her own magic: as the water sprayed out, she caught it and separated each burst into separate floating bubbles. "What are my choices here?" Queenie asked Flavia. "Love-me-not isn't going to get us very far as a defensive weapon."

"Love, love-me-not, hate, truth, life, wisdom, know-not, oblivion, youth, transformation, undoing and the water of worlds," Flavia rattled off.

Queenie frowned at the philtres. "I can tell which ones don't belong together, well enough to keep them separate. But otherwise, I can't tell which philtre is which. Will it make a terrible mess if I throw them all at once?"

"Petronella," gasped Lady Mortmain. "You don't know what you are doing. Trust your Aunt Elspeth.

We can have *everything*. I'll make you my heir.
Wouldn't you like to be a princess of the realm?"

Queenie screwed her face up. "No, thank you.
Have you seen what they do to princesses of the realm?
Most of them are married, cursed, or dead."

Another wall fell away from the bronze edifice as
Rinaldo wrought his destruction. More water gushed.
Queenie seized these new philtres, separated the liquid
into further floating bubbles, and added them to her
collection, which bobbed above head-height. She had
seven now, of the twelve philtres. "I know exactly what
I'm doing," she said primly. "I'm rather good at this,
Auntie. If you paid the slightest bit of attention to me,
you would know all about my expertise at transporting
liquids without test tubes. Tell me, is there any reason I
shouldn't hurl these at you and my false uncle over there,
to allow Flavia and Rinaldo to escape your horrid house?"

Lady Mortmain's mouth opened, but nothing
emerged. The sight of all those philtre bubbles clearly
astonished her.

*Love, love-me-not, hate, truth, life, wisdom, know-
not, oblivion, youth, transformation, undoing and the
water of worlds.*

Bubble after bubble of philtre joined the collection
over their heads. The rest were contained within the
collapsing fountain, under the control of its creator:
Rinaldo Device.

"I have a reason," said Quicksilver. She began to

stalk towards Queenie, slowly but relentlessly, step by step. "You can't kill me, little girl. If I die here, I wake up in my own body back on the Isle of Faerie, and you have a dead uncle lying on the floor. So what exactly do I have to lose?"

Queenie hurled a bubble at her. It smashed wetly into her face, drenching Lord Perrault's glasses. Quicksilver froze in shock for a moment, and then reached up and took off the wet spectacles. The first person that her silver eyes focused upon was Flavia, and she did not look away.

Flavia stared back warily. *Not the philtre of love, please. Anything but that.*

Quicksilver took another step, this time in Flavia's direction. Queenie hurled another bubble. Quicksilver swayed, and crumpled wetly to the floor.

"I think that one might have been oblivion," said Queenie, biting her lips. "Or perhaps I hit him too hard."

"Just hard enough," said Rinaldo. With a street magician's flourish, he freed the final wall of the bronze fountain, collapsing it inwards with a mighty twist. Queenie caught more water in floating bubbles. With her own version of flourish, she cast them all in the general direction of her Aunt Elspeth, slowing them in a threatening cloud above her head.

The enchantress stood very still.

The Gloucestercator made a loud dinging noise.

There was a wheezing, whirring sound, and the door rolled open in fits and starts.

"Ay-ay, what's all this, then, are we trashing the place?" called a voice abundant with cheer and charm. "Save some for me."

Flavia saw Rinaldo's whole demeanor change. A tension melted from his shoulders.

Orlando Device strolled into the attic as if he owned the place, his clothes filthy with dust and soot, and a cat under each arm. He surveyed the destruction before him. "Nice work, Professor," he said with pride.

"Where the hellfire were you?" Rinaldo roared.

"Getting acquainted with the elaborate maze of chimneys and heating duct systems in the middle of this house — and in case you were wondering, yes, the ducts hate us too. Got the cat, though. And a spare." Spying Flavia and Queenie, Orlando gave each of them a gentlemanly bob of his head. "Ladies." At the sight of Lady Mortmain surrounded by bubbles of philtre, he smirked. "My dear madam. How is *your* evening going?"

Flavia stared at the cats. One of them was the spiky, impolite yellow creature that had led her such a dance early this evening. It seemed a terribly long time ago. The other was a familiar placid tabby. "Dash? Is that you?"

The tabby tumbled out of Orlando's grip and transformed into the young lord and heir of the Gloucester family, in bright striped pyjamas. "Queenie, guess what?" he gabbled at his sister. "I was in a *chimney*! I went all the way up! It was splendid."

Queenie Gloucester burst into tears. The floating bubbles of philtre above Lady Mortmain's head wobbled, but did not fall.

"What did I miss?" asked Orlando Device.

The twisted and damaged remains of the bronze fountain shuddered. As if in response, the real house vibrated around them.

"Don't worry," said Rinaldo. "There's plenty of damage for you to get in on."

"You, all of you!" snarled Lady Mortmain. "Jesting and mocking as if I am here for your entertainment. I am not going to be stopped by a gaggle of children and conjurers!"

"Who are we to stop you becoming queen?" Flavia replied in a dry voice.

Orlando cracked up laughing. "It's a long time since anyone's called me a conjurer," he spluttered. "Where are my silk scarves and playing cards?"

"Don't move, Aunt Elspeth," said Queenie, working to keep her voice steady. The bubbles of philtre shimmered over Lady Mortmain, drawing down to her.

"Wretched brat, you dare to threaten me with your schoolroom magic?" Lady Elspeth howled. "You may be immune to my powers, but I can still do damage to the floorboards under your feet!" She pointed one arm at the twisted bronze remains of the philtre fountain, still gushing water in flat puddles across the attic floor.

It all happened so fast. Flavia was pounced upon by Orlando, of all people, who knocked her against the nearest wall. The yellow cat took the opportunity to break free of Orlando's arm, skidding under a chair and vanishing from sight. Flavia felt rather than saw Rinaldo command the bronze into the air, forming a protective wall between the children and their enraged enchantress aunt.

Vines and flowers burst out of the attic walls and floorboards, out of the fountain itself, growing impossibly large and green and hissing with magic as they smashed through wood and plaster and bronze. Water exploded everywhere, evaporating into a cloud of steamy fog that enveloped Rinaldo and the children, Lady Mortmain, and even the unconscious Quicksilver/Lord Perrault.

They were gone in an eye blink.

How?

Flavia struggled to her feet, gasping for air. Orlando leaped up beside her, brushing dust and pieces of exploded plant from his suit. She stumbled, her feet making the damaged floor creak alarmingly. She could see a wreckage of bronze and plants and dripping water, but no people. No Rinaldo, and no children. No *cats*.

The attic was empty, except for herself and

Orlando Device, and the lingering scent of grass in the air.

She had failed.

Flavia's feet slid from under her. She felt Orlando catch her around her waist, steadying her. When she finally dared look at his face, she saw a grim expression on his pretty face. "What exactly," he asked in a low voice, "Did that witch do to my brother?"

Love, love-me-not, hate, truth, life, wisdom, know-not, oblivion, youth, transformation, undoing and the water of worlds.

"The water of worlds," Flavia gasped. She recognised the smell that lingered from the cloud of steam: a scent she knew only from her dreams, the smell of damp grass and moss and acorn wine.

"She's transported them somewhere," Orlando said, trying to understand. "Are they all gambolling around the Forest of Arden like something out of a rural ballad? The heroes never have happy endings in those stories! Especially knights who mess around with fountains and philtres and enchantresses."

"Not Arden," said Flavia, breathing deeply. Oh, that scent. She longed for it. "In the tales of Chivalry, the water of worlds was always thought to be the most dangerous of the philtres, because it could be used to travel between the mortal world and that of Faerie."

Orlando blew out a very long breath. "All of them?" he said after a moment. "Even the cat?"

"Even the cat," Flavia said heavily.

Orlando used several words that Flavia had never learned in her childhood.

"Stop that," she said in her governess voice. "We must think. What do we have to work with? No more philtres." The floorboards were soaking wet, the last remains of philtres all muddled together.

Orlando turned to at her, his dark eyes gleaming. "I took a second set of water samples when we were in Arden. Hid them where Lady Sourdrawers would never think to look."

Flavia nodded. It was a start, at least. It was hope. "Where did you hide them?"

"Buckingham Palace," said Orlando.

She stared at him, waiting for the laugh to show he was teasing, but his face remained deadly serious. "Oh, you mean it. What is the obsession you two have with that place?"

"On my oath I mean it. Best hiding place in the Britannian Empire."

"But... aren't you running away from the Queen and her family?"

"I didn't say I was going to ring the doorbell and ask permission." Orlando held out a hand to her. "Let's get out of this damned house and grab those philtres. It's the only way to get them all back. My brother, your children. The cat."

Put like that, how could Flavia possibly argue? Very slowly, she placed her gloved hand in his. "Fine.

If that's our only option, I suppose we'd better go... to Buckingham Palace."

As if this night could possibly get any more strange.

Lady Mortmain's final desperate spell had awoken most of the household of Number 12, Actaeon Place. There was noise everywhere — shuffles and cries and consternation.

Flavia and Orlando managed to escape it all. The Earl was asleep, back in bed after the compulsion that Lady Mortmain had laid upon him. They checked on him as they emerged from the Gloustercator.

The house itself was shocked enough by the events that it did not try to hinder Orlando's path. Perhaps it was pleased to see him leave — or perhaps it cared less about hating him now that its mistress was no longer in residence. Flavia held his hand regardless, not wanting to risk it. It reminded her of how she had led Rinaldo through the house safely, only a short while ago.

They walked down the main staircase, and out the front door, for all the world as if they were members of the family. No one stopped them. They only paused only to help themselves to two enormous coats from the butler's alcove.

Flavia could hear a commotion coming from the kitchens below. The death of Mrs Brundage must have been discovered. She felt a twinge of obligation to stay and help, though she knew that it impossible. She felt guilty about the coats, too, but not so guilty that she didn't accept a splendid foxfur hat that Orlando handed to her with a bow of his head.

There was a horrible kind of freedom in walking away from the Gloucester family in the midst of a spectacular crisis.

Walking smartly away from Actaeon Place in the dead of night with her arm tucked into that of Mr Orlando Device at least meant that Flavia would not have to explain the disappearance of the two children under her charge.

(It was important not to dwell too deeply upon the loss of those children; the very thought of it made her breath come too fast and her chest clench in panic.)

Flavia set her mind to the job at hand. Buckingham Palace first. Then Faerie. They had a plan.

A Thames fog rolled along the streets, thick and porous. The night was green around them, rather than black. As Flavia matched Orlando's stride with her own quick steps, she allowed the illusion to slide off her skin.

If fog could turn the world green, she could be green too.

Orlando glanced over at her and grinned, snugging her arm more tightly into his. "That suits you," he said.

"I like to think so," said Flavia, feeling reckless.

It was not snowing in London tonight, but something about the chill in the air signalled that it was coming: the cold would close in around them hard and fast, and the sky would fill with swirling white. Flavia was grateful for the coat and the cozy fur hat as she walked briskly along.

She had been aware, in a vague sort of geographical way, that Belgravia was quite near Buckingham Palace, but she had avoided leaving the house except for the excursion to Penge. As it turned out, they needed to cross only two or three large blocks of white pavements, terraced houses and grey-green fog before the tangible presence of the palace's surrounding parks hit her magic with the weight of a redwood trunk to the stomach.

The iron and steel of London fell away, leaving nothing in her head but an awareness of grass and twiggy branches and the blissful, blissful scent of living things that grew.

"So beautiful," Flavia breathed, gazing through the railings. Even in the darkness, she could feel the majesty of these gardens beyond the metal spikes.

Orlando shuffled his feet uncomfortably. "It's just a palace."

"I meant the park," she teased as they strolled alongside iron railings. Their proximity itched at her, but there was so much delicious greenery beyond that it did not bother her unduly. "You're awfully cavalier about palaces. Are you certain you're not a prince in disguise?"

Orlando laughed in a short bark. "Palaces have

hardly any princes in them, when weighed against the rest of the residents. Hundreds of servants, ministers, advisors, artisans and other hangers-on, all running around like headless chickens to obey the whims of the handful of royals in the centre of it all. As if they are more important than anyone else in the world."

"Of course," Flavia said softly. "You were a Royal Engineer. Did you *live* here?"

Orlando looked up, and briefly trailed a finger along the iron railing of the park. "Half my life. Most of my life that I care to remember."

"If you are in so much trouble with the Queen," Flavia said after a moment's thought. "Why did you hide the philtres here?"

He shrugged. "Rinaldo didn't trust Lady Mortmain, and we figured she was unlikely to scale an eight foot iron fence to check whether I'd been stashing secrets in the trees."

"I can't scale the fence, either," Flavia said briskly. No time for sentiment. They had a rescue to plan. "Too much iron is uncomfortable for me, and I am not going to risk having one of those spikes draw my blood. I'll wait on the street."

"You can't wait on the street," Orlando said with a mock-gasp. "Passers by will think you're a lady of fallen virtue." He reached out and took hold of one of the metal railings. "Luckily for us, not every magic-worker in this country is at the mercy of iron."

As Flavia stared, the entire fence bent and twisted,

the railings giving way like ribbons fluttering in the night breeze. Orlando swept them aside, presenting Flavia with a civilised entrance to the palace park. "After you, Miss Wednesday," he said with a polite flourish.

She squeezed through, gritting her teeth against the presence of the iron. It was worth the discomfort. On the other side of the fence, she was welcomed by the staggering scent of oak trees, winter roses, and acres of grass. The palace, a shadowy shape some significant distance from where they stood, was of no interest to her. "Good trees," Flavia breathed.

Orlando finished repairing the gap he had made in the fence. "Glad you approve," he said, taking her hand. "I'll show you my favourite."

A few minutes later, Flavia found herself standing beside a hollowed tree in the foggy park, standing lookout while Orlando Device lowered himself inside said favourite tree. "You had better not be sneaking off down some elaborate network of secret tunnels," she said irritably. Her experience of recent days suggested that such a thing was not only possible, but extremely likely. "I don't fancy having to explain to the guards why I'm here. I can't leave without your magic."

Orlando said something placating from within the tree, but it was muffled. Flavia tucked her cold hands inside the sleeves of the heavy coat she wore, and waited.

A lantern flared suddenly, in the foggy darkness.

"Orlando," Flavia hissed. "Someone's coming." There was nowhere to hide except behind the tree, and that felt silly. She stood her ground, toning the greenness of her skin back beneath its usual illusion as the lantern moved towards her at a rush, and a light was cast abruptly upon her face.

"Good evening," Flavia said in a small voice.

The owner of the lantern was not a groundskeeper or footman as she had expected, but a young lady around Flavia's age. She had dark eyes and hair, and a pale face sticking out from a voluminous hood. *Beautiful*, was Flavia's first thought. *Angry*, was her second.

The girl gaped at Flavia for a moment, then turned her attention to the tree.

"Orlando Device," she snapped in an accent so aristocratic it was almost otherworldly. "Did you think I wouldn't set proximity sparks to stop you sneaking back like a thief in the night? If you don't come out of that tree this minute, my mother will have you drawn and quartered!"

There were some shuffling sounds, and Orlando's face appeared from within the branches, his rumpled black hair even more of a wild disaster than usual. The lantern light blazed up at him, catching him full in the face.

Then he smiled, that careless, charming smile of his. "Ygraine, love. May I introduce you to Miss Flavia Wednesday? Flavia, this is her royal highness, the Duchess of Cornwall, one of my very best friends. I know you know are going to get along famously."

"You maniac," said the princess between gritted teeth. "Never mind pretending to have good manners. Get your arse down here and explain what in hellfire you have done with my husband!"

END

Afterword

Thank you so much for reading the second novella in the Sparks & Philtres series! Flavia, the Gloucester family and the Extraordinary and Miraculous Device Brothers (not to mention a certain Princess Y) will return in...

LAND GLORIOUS
(SPARKS & PHILTRES #3)

A Thrilling Tale of Mortals Lost in Faerie, Lovers Bespelled, Philtrecraft Unfiltered, Two Queens Battling To the Death in a House of Flowers and Sorrowful Secrets Sensationally Spilled...

I would be delighted if you chose to review this book at your book vendor of choice.

Now read on for a bonus story...

Bonus Story

A Tale of Two Worthy Orphans

The boy had been born in Britannia, as far as he knew.
He was the only brown child in the Duchess of Bath
Institution for Worthy Orphans. He had not been
allowed to keep his original name, Rajendra, which he
once found written in the neat book that Mrs Hopkins
kept in her office.

He was Richard now. It was common for Mrs
Hopkins to change the names of the orphans if they
sounded too grand or foreign or odd. Little Evanna
with the freckled nose was renamed Annie when she
arrived, and she cried about it for days, protesting that
Eirish names were good enough for the Queen and the
royal princesses. She was slapped for that, and Mrs
Hopkins informed them all in her chill, dark voice, that
what was right and proper for the Queen of Britannia's
family was not for the likes of them.

Annie, she went on to say, was a good and honest servant's name, and a position as a servant in a good household was the best that any of the Worthy Orphans could hope for.

That explained some things, though it didn't make sense that it was all right for everyone to call the boy Richard, after an old Britannian king, but Evanna could not keep a name that she shared with one of the princesses.

The boy learned not to protest being Richard instead of Rajendra, and then not to ask questions in general, because Mrs Hopkins was quicker to smack him than the other boys. She would also make cutting remarks that were worse than the smacks. He dug a place inside himself, gathering observations about the world and his place in it.

He learned that Rajendra was an Indian name, and that India belonged to the Britannian Empire now, but was very far away. Despite reading every book, pamphlet and newspaper journal that passed through the building, that was all that he knew about himself for much of his childhood.

The patrons of the Institution, the Duke and Duchess of Bath, would visit once a year, bringing toys and books for the children. One year, they actually brought a lavishly illustrated book of Indian fairy tales that Richard pored over with delight, though he knew the binding was too rich and they would not be allowed to keep it. Sure enough, within a day, the book had 'disappeared' into the drawer where Mrs Hopkins kept things that were too good for children. It was always the same drawer, though enough things had gone into it over the years that it should have burst off its hinges by now.

Richard learned to appreciate the books that had ripped pages or faded covers: they never made their way into the drawer. There was a battered atlas in the common room, which was mostly used for games or chocking up the wobbly table. He spent many hours quietly examining the large and sprawling country of India, learning the names of towns and villages and rivers, searching for anything that might feel familiar.

It never did.

He worked on not being noticed, and making himself useful. If they were destined to be servants, there was no point in being a bad one. The only servants Richard had ever met, apart from the smooth-faced footmen that accompanied the Duke and Duchess of Bath, were the cook and scullery maid who worked for Mrs Hopkins. They hated her as much as she hated the children. They were all terribly rude to each other, which made the kitchen a miserable place.

He would be better than that, when he was in service. He had a talent for making his face blankly polite even when he felt very angry, and it seemed to Richard that he might make a jolly good footman, perhaps even a butler someday. He wasn't sure what a footman did other than packing and unpacking gentleman's trunks, but it seemed like the sort of future that would occasionally allow a day off, which would be an improvement on his current life.

He made the error of mentioning his ambition to some of the other Worthy Orphan boys, who promptly dropped the game of wooden soldiers they had been playing, and jeered at him for a full hour at thinking he could rise to the ranks of footman.

Perhaps there was another kind of servant who fixed things, and made them work better, while remaining discreetly out of public view. That was a job he could see himself enjoying. If Richard was allowed to fix things, he mightn't even want a day off.

Everything changed when the new boy arrived. Richard was tinkering with the clock in the common room when Charlie said, "Another of your lot came in last night. Got a brother, have you?"

"He looks ever so smart," said Betsy, who was the nicest of the girls and could be counted on for a game of marbles most of the time. "Wearing a suit like a proper gentleman."

"Maybe he's here to adopt us," jibed Annie, and they all laughed.

When the new boy was brought to them by Mrs

Hopkins, he wore a plain cotton shirt like the rest of them, and a pair of old trousers that Charlie had worn before he grew out of them. The fine suit had obviously disappeared into that drawer of hers.

This boy wasn't Indian, as Richard had hoped from what Charlie said. He looked more like the Chinamen who worked at the fish market near the little church they all walked to on Sundays. He must be from that expanse on the atlas that their schoolteacher called the Mysterious Orient. Richard had always thought it odd that one place should have a name meaning East — after all, everything was East of somewhere, except perhaps the North Pole.

Names were important. He had learned that lesson already.

"Children, this is James," said Mrs Hopkins briskly. "Make him welcome." She always said that about the new ones, and rarely waited around long enough to see if the order was obeyed.

Before Mrs Hopkins could withdraw, the new boy coughed politely. He looked so odd, with black hair sticking up in all directions as if he had never combed it in his life. Richard was not sure if you could get your hair that wild by simply not combing it — surely you had to *work* to achieve such a maddening effect.

"My name," said the boy when he was sure he had everybody's attention, "is Othello Orlando Lancelot the Third. Not James. I don't think I know anyone called James."

In the shocked silence that followed, only Annie giggled and snorted. The rest were caught in horrified awe at the utter cheek of him.

Mrs Hopkins gave the boy an affronted look. "James," she repeated. "Your name is James. Don't forget again."

The boy rolled his eyes at her, and she boxed his ears so fast he didn't see her coming. As James dropped to the ground with a low cry, Richard retreated behind the other children, not wanting the troublemaker to see him, or to assume they had anything in common.

They must never, ever become friends.

James made no further attempts to insist he was Othello Orlando or any other outlandish name. Richard was surprised that he gave in so easily.

After that rocky start, the Chinese boy genuinely seemed to enjoy being a Worthy Orphan. He was friendly and cheerful with the other children, enjoying nothing more than to entertain an audience. Richard had been right not to befriend him — James was the very opposite of the grave young boy who hid behind a book whenever possible.

But of course, it couldn't be that easy.

"Why don't you ever speak to me?" James asked one day. Richard had been reading about knights and enchantresses in a corner while the rest of the children played castles at the other end of the common room.

Richard blinked for a moment, startled. "I don't talk to anyone much."

"So, you're *not* scared of being friends?"

Pretty much everything about James scared Richard. "I'm not scared of anything," he said, hoping to be left alone.

"You should be," said James, bouncing on his heels as if even this brief conversation was too much staying still. "Some of that lot say awful things about you when you're not around. I once saw a couple of white boys about as big as that Charlie beating and kicking another lad in the street, because he wasn't like them."

Richard shivered. "I'm not like *you*," he said, and turned his back on the new boy.

Sometime later, he heard the girls pestering James for a story. James began a long, elaborate and obviously made-up-on-the-spot tale about how he had once travelled with a Romani troupe across Europe: caravans, greasepaint, silk costumes and an elephant. It was quite the thrilling adventure. Richard buried himself in a book, head down so that no one could tell that he was listening to every word.

～

He dreamed of India often. The India of Richard's dreams was made up from pictures in books, and half-imagined details that didn't quite fit together. He always woke feeling unsatisfied and angry, as if something important had been taken away all over again. Anger was something to be pressed down deep in his stomach where no one could ever know about it.

Boys like him could not afford to get angry. He needed to stick to the basics: say please and thank you, stay quiet, keep out of trouble.

No one had ever conveyed this philosophy to James. After only a couple of months as a Worthy Orphan, the new boy was legendary for his impertinence. James missed suppers. He had his ears boxed or his hand strapped at least once a week, and his mouth washed out with soap once a fort-night. Finally he did something so terrible (apparently) that he was actually whipped, and sent to sleep two nights in the coal shed. Rumours about what he had actually done (or said) to deserve this went wild around the orphanage, but all a tight-lipped Mrs Hopkins would say were the words 'gross insubordination.'

Richard and Annie were on kitchen duty on the Sunday morning when James was finally let out of the coal shed. They were scrubbing the breakfast bowls and forks and spoons because it was the scullery maid's half-day. Both Richard and Annie had a good view of the yard when Mrs Hopkins let James out, directing him to wash himself at the pump.

It was chilly in the kitchen, even with the fire going. Richard could see James' breath steam in the morning air as he pumped water over his arms and legs, wetting his filthy coal-streaked shirt and trousers.

"I like him," said Annie in a thoughtful voice. "He's funny."

Richard shook his head. "If only he could behave himself. He's stupid not to try."

She flicked a bit of greasy water at him. "Don't you ever get tired of being good all the time? I wish I was brave like James."

"Then you'd be the one being whipped," Richard said with an air of doom.

Annie frowned, and he felt bad about saying it. To cheer her up, Richard did his favourite trick for her. He had been practicing it for ages. Carefully, he balanced a spoon upon its tip end on the window ledge, then balanced another on top of it. He got the tower as high as six spoons, each balancing perfectly upon each other like they were one big spoon.

Annie's smile was worth the effort it took to keep the spoons balancing perfectly in the air. Her smile was better than anything.

Richard let the spoons fall into the water, and when he looked up he saw that a dripping wet James was watching him silently through the kitchen window.

That night, Richard heard someone crying in the far bed of the boys' dorm. Boys who cried never wanted to be noticed. You were supposed to lie still and not acknowledge you could hear. He found himself slipping out from under the starchy sheets and creeping along to where the new boy slept. "You all right?" he whispered in the darkness.

A very long pause. "I hate this place," James whispered back.

"You only think that because you get in trouble all the time," said Richard, sitting on the floor beside the bed, his back against the wall.

James turned so that his eyes were peering at Richard from under his sheet. "How can *you* not get into trouble? So many rules to remember, and they hate it when we think for ourselves. You think all the time."

Richard was startled that James had noticed. "I keep my thinking inside my head," he said primly. "You should try it some time."

James laughed quietly. "I liked your trick with the spoons," he added. "How d'you do it?"

Richard smiled modestly. "I'm good at balancing."

James pushed back his sheet so that his whole head now poked out from under the covers. "You don't actually think you were balancing those spoons, do you?"

"Of course."

"Nuh-uh. It was magic."

Richard scoffed at that. "No, it wasn't."

"You're a spark, that's what you are. Do it again."

"No!" Richard hissed. He felt daft for coming all the way over here. James didn't sound miserable anymore, and they would really catch it if any of the adults found Richard out of bed. He didn't want trouble. "I don't have any spoons here."

"Steal some combs and things from the girls' dorm."

"No!" Richard was scandalised. "Anyway, it only works with metal."

"Interesting," James said, sounding like their school-teacher. "Hairpins. I bet Betsy or Annie would give you some if you asked. They like you."

"I'm going back to bed," Richard huffed.

Nothing good would come of being friends with this new boy. He must stay away from him, or suffer the consequences.

"Where are you really from?" Betsy asked the Chinese boy the next day, after lessons. James had received the strap for having a smart mouth, and now sat in the common room, wriggling his hands to get the feeling back into them.

Richard tried not to be jealous that Betsy was taking an interest in James. Betsy had always been Richard's friend. She and Annie were the only ones he could trust to talk to sometimes, and they never called him names.

James gave her a long, measuring look. "I travelled with the Romani for years," he said. "But I was never one of them. I was discovered as an orphan on the streets of Peking, with naught but a gold rattle and a silk blanket to my name."

Charlie snorted and shoved at James as he went past. "We're all orphans," he said, and called James one of the names that Richard hated most.

Annie, sitting a bit back from the others, had the brains to be skeptical about anything that came out of James' mouth: she'd heard a lot of his stories by now. Like Richard, she paid attention to the details enough to know they often crossed over each other. "A silk blanket?" she said, raising her eyebrows.

"It was orange with a turquoise trim," said James, warming to his theme. "Everyone in Peking wears silk, it's so hot there. The Romani who found me thought I was the son of a prince, for the fine clothes I wore and that rattle. They stole me away, planning to collect a ransom."

"A gold rattle," Betsy repeated, her eyes shining. She never questioned the stories, no matter how many times she heard James spout utter nonsense.

All of the Worthy Orphans told stories about where they came from. Everyone except Richard, who had never been able to decide which of the many cities in the India section of the atlas he liked best. Betsy was convinced she was the illegitimate daughter of a duchess who fell in love with a footman and was cast out for her sins. Edward told tales about the orphanage he was in before this one, where they were given gruel once a day and sent out pickpocketing.

James was better at stories than most. Today, as he launched into his tale of love and loss and travelling theatre and the silk-strewn streets of Peking, he had them all in the palm of his hand.

Richard did not begrudge James the lies. He had plenty of his own, after all. He just hugged them to his heart instead of spilling them out in public.

He was entirely unprepared when James called across the common room: "What about you, Richard? Where are you from?"

Startled to be addressed, Richard thought back to that much-pored-over atlas. "Bangalore," he said, picking the city he had read about most recently. "In India. My father was..." He thought desperately of what kind of people made things, or fixed things. "A carpenter. He came here to work in a Britannian factory and earn money for our family. But they all died." He tried to look sad.

James said nothing, but looked slightly impressed. Richard wondered if it was because he believed the story, or because he had guessed Richard had thought up the lie. Either option made him feel cross. "What happened to your Romani theatre troupe?" he challenged. "Why aren't you still with them?"

"Plague," said James, watching Richard carefully. It was if only the two of them were in the room together. "We played Shakespeare to a crowd outside Paris, but the audience were coughing so much they could hardly hear the words. Then the next day,

Carlotta Maria had the cough, and Marco, and the rest of them. They dropped like flies. Three days later, they were all dead but me."

A few of the younger children sidled in, listening. They knew a good show when they heard one.

"How'd you get to Britannia from Paris?" asked little Edward.

James hesitated only briefly. "Caught a lift with a Cornish fisherman. Nice old fellow. Didn't understand a word he said, except that he called me Ching Chong and thought he was *hilarious*. His wife cooked herring soup."

It was in the details, Richard marvelled. That was the trick to a good lie. James was a master at it, and he captivated his audience every time.

That night, after Mrs Hopkins blew out the lamp to signal it was time for the boys to go to sleep, Richard found a handful of spiky hairpins under his pillow. He ignored them as long as he could, but the nearness of the metal gave him a headache.

As soon as he heard enough snoring to be certain that the room was generally asleep, he sneaked over to James' bed, determined to return the dratted things.

"Go on, then," James whispered, peering out from beneath the thin blanket with those piercing eyes of his. "Bet you can't."

Richard was going to throw the hairpins at him, but the dare gave him pause. He knelt down, and placed one pin on its end upon the floor. Carefully, he balanced a second on top of it, and then another, until he had a dozen of them forming a slender and wavering tower which was higher than James' bed.

James stared at it in wonder. "Now do a person," he urged.

Richard had never done that before, but the suggestion made him realise exactly how it could be managed. He drew down the tower of pins and placed two on the ground for legs, meeting at the top, then another for the body, and two for arms. He bent one around in a circle and placed it on the top as the head. The tapped the little hairpin person and made it walk, then dance.

James breathed in an odd way, his eyes fixed to the tiny performance. Slowly, he reached down a hand to touch it just as Richard had, lightly on the head.

A warm breeze blew around Richard's face. The hairpin person grew silvery flesh, rounding out as if its head and limbs were made of clay. It had a face now, a real face like a jack-in-the-box or a toy soldier, and it danced with tiny perfect shoes upon its feet.

"You made it real," he whispered.

James smiled, the joy in his face almost lighting up the dark dormitory. "We made it real," he replied. "Your magic and mine. We did it together."

They were friends after that. Now that Richard knew about the strange metal magic that flowed within him, he was willing to do anything to do it again, and again.

Even if that meant letting himself getting attached to James, and all the trouble he caused.

It was nearly a year before their experiments got them into proper hot water. It began on a warm Saturday when the Duke and Duchess of Bath came to visit in that odd carriage of theirs, the one that made a humming noise and ran without horses. Richard had been longing to get a closer look at it, but Mrs Hopkins always had a job for him on the ducal days, and he'd never had a chance to get near.

Today, the Duke and Duchess had brought one of their nieces — a royal princess, with dark hair and a sulky face — to see the Institution for Worthy Orphans. Mrs Hopkins was so overwhelmed by the royal honour that she got quite distracted with tea and scones, and forgot to give Richard a task.

He caught James' eye as he made his surreptitious way through the kitchens, and the two of them snuck out and around to the garage.

"Smells funny," said James in a mutter.

"It's warm," said Richard, one hand trailing across the polished wood chassis.

There was no sign of a driver. Most times, if a servant or two came along with the Duke and Duchess, they'd have been in the kitchens angling for a hot cuppa by now. Richard had seen no one.

"What do you think makes it run?" he asked, though he could already feel the tug of metal and magic pulling at him from under the bonnet.

"Optimism and cabbage scraps," said James promptly. A pair of riding goggles hung idly from the wheel, and his fingers reached for them longingly before he snatched his own hand back. "Want to go for a spin?"

"We couldn't!"

"Reckon we could."

"They'd kill us," said Richard, sick with envy that James could even speak the fantasy aloud.

"Worth it," said James with a wicked grin.

Richard's gaze was caught by a trail of oil running out of the front of the chassis. "Something's wrong there."

"Think we can fix it?" James had to know that the chance of getting his hands on the internal works – of fixing the horseless carriage himself – was a far more exciting temptation to Richard than driving it.

"Let's have a quick look," he said, and opened the catch to flip up the metal lid of the carriage before he could change his mind.

A little tinkering wouldn't hurt anyone.

An hour or so later, they were both streaked with oil and sweat and smelled like stale magic, but oh, they knew how the engine worked now, and they had managed to tweak some of the inner tubes between them to work more efficiently and cut down on oil leakage.

Richard's head was bursting with ways to improve the design, that he did not hear the Duke approach until a loud, Germanian-accented voice bellowed: "I appear to have picked up a couple of engineers, *nein*?"

James' eyes bulged, but he recovered quickly. "We've fixed your oil problem," he announced, hands thumbing his belt. "The tubes were too short, so the steel enchantments rubbed up against each other, causing friction. It should be smoother now, won't spring as many leaks."

Richard hyperventilated quietly, wondering if he could actually crawl inside the magical engine to hide or possibly die.

"Indeed," said the Duke, examining their work with a professional eye. Everyone knew the Duke of Bath was in love with inventing. Had he built this marvel on his own? "Excellent work, my fine fellows. The charms you placed on the steam core are primitive but effective. What methodology did you follow?"

Richard blinked. He felt calmer now that he knew he wasn't about to shouted at, and there was a conversation about engines in the offing. "Methodology, my lord?"

"*Ja*, what technique did you use to ground the

magic in the metal? Which book did you learn it from?"

Richard gaped at the thought that they might have been supplied with magical books at any point in their education. "We don't," he said, and stopped.

"We've never read any books about magic," James said bluntly. "They never give them to us."

"Well," said the Duke, stroking his prodigious beard. "We shall have to do something about that."

Richard had still not recovered from this conversation, hours later when James climbed into his bed so they could debrief about the marvellous horseless carriage all over again. Richard could hardly bring himself to talk about it.

"Do you think he's really going to bring us books?" James asked finally.

"Don't get your hopes up," Richard sighed. "We can't trust grown ups, you know that. We can't trust anyone."

The fact that he trusted *James* was hard enough on his heart, because it was something that could be taken away from him, and he did not know how he could manage being alone again.

"It's not like we have anything to lose," James grunted, elbowing him a little as he got comfy.

"They might separate us," Richard said flatly. "Had you thought of that?"

James was silent.

"Anyway," Richard added. "If he did bring us

books about magic, she would only snatch them away. Into that drawer of hers."

"I hate that drawer," groaned James.

Mrs Hopkins was not a pleasant woman, in nature or appearance. She had a pallid face and a sour expression, particularly in the presence of children. You could not imagine a person less suited to running an orphanage, particularly an orphanage boasting the Duke and Duchess of Bath as its esteemed benefactors: a soft-hearted couple of toffs who insisted on the importance of regular schooling, and liked to see rosy cheeks, clean hands and chubby tummies when they arrived to inspect.

This coddling attitude enraged Mrs Hopkins. She employed all manner of leave-no-marks punishments when a ducal visit was expected.

Thank goodness she had never learned about the business with the carriage, and the Duke's special interest in his two 'engineers'.

Her rage knew no bounds, however, when she caught James and Richard in the coal shed with the fully working clockwork steam train they had constructed from scraps of tin and bent hairpins. It was a fort-night before the Duke and Duchess were next due, and thus she felt no compunction about dragging them into the courtyard by their ears, and whipping their backs with a knotted length of rope.

The other children clustered in the kitchen, peeping over the sill to watch as the boys gritted their teeth against every lash of pain.

It hurt more than anything Richard had ever felt before. He tried not to cry, but he was a mess by the end of it, and could not pretend otherwise. James made no noise. His face was flat and empty like the surface of a stone.

In all the commotion, Mrs Hopkins never stopped to ask exactly how it was that two boys had managed to create such a complex and wondrous piece of magical machinery out of scraps and metal. She wasn't paid to think, nor to care about how they had done it as long as they knew *never to do it again*.

The other Worthy Orphans had figured it out, though, and they regarded both boys with fear and awe after that.

No one said the word out loud where grownups might hear, but they whispered it sometimes to each other, and didn't even make it sound like it was a bad word.

Sparks.

～

The Duke of Bath arrived without notice, a day after the whipping. He took tea with Mrs Hopkins and nodded and smiled politely at the fresh-faced children who waited upon them. To the horror of Mrs Hopkins, he asked particularly to see Richard and James.

"The boys have a talent for mechanics," he informed her in his thick accent. "I am thinking of bringing them into my personal household as apprentices."

On a normal day, Mrs Hopkins might have preened like a peacock at the thought of offloading two of her charges to a good position... a Royal position, no less. But she was uncomfortably aware of the stripes across the boys' shoulders; the broken skin that would be visible if anyone checked below their shirt collars. Her hand shook a little as she lowered her teacup.

"If you want an apprentice for your driver, your grace, you couldn't do better than our Charlie. A big lad, he's ready to go out into the world and make something of himself."

The Duke smiled. "I want Richard and James," he said with polite certainty.

When the boys were brought to him, freshly washed and shivering, the Duke examined them with a frown beneath his enormous beard. They made a good face of it, the two of them, pretending no discomfort as they sat gingerly on Mrs Hopkins' good chairs and were handed cups of tea.

"Well, young men," said the Duke. "You like to fix things, *ja*? I would like to know whether you also have the talent for construction."

He knew, Richard realised. Someone — one of the servants — must have sent a message to him. About the train, perhaps, or the hairpins and the forks... It was all too much of a coincidence.

Then, he glanced over at James and wondered if it had been the servants at all. Had James himself somehow got word to the Duke of Bath about their magical experiments?

James brimmed over with excitement. "Would you like to see our train, sir?"

Mrs Hopkins' mouth went so thin you could hardly see it anymore, but she could not stop this now. She had spent two days shouting at the servants to break the train set apart, but not one of them had been able to figure out how to do it.

"I would like that very much," said the Duke of Bath, sounding satisfied. "Then after that, we shall pack your things. I am taking you both to live in my household."

"Where is that?" asked Richard in a small voice, because he liked to know things, and it wasn't as if the furious, vibrating Mrs Hopkins could get any angrier at this point.

"Why," said the Duke with a twitch of his handlebar moustache. "London, of course. Buckingham Palace, to be precise. My wife, the Duchess, is a beloved cousin of the Queen. We are all very great friends."

Buckingham Palace.

Mrs Hopkins looked so pale, you could ink lines across her face. *I must not whip the orphans* would have been particularly pertinent, if a little too late.

~

"We should be Orlando and Rinaldo," James decided as the horseless coach rattled along, delivering them to their new life. They sat in the spacious back seat, giddy with delight as the Duke steered them to their new home. There had never been a driver, they realised now. Of course, if the Duke had built this contraption, he would wish to drive it himself.

Richard stared at James. "We should *what*?"

"We're on our way now. With the patronage of the Royal Family, living at Buckingham Palace... we can be extraordinary. But there's nothing extraordinary about names like James and Richard, is there? It's not as if we have names from Peking or Bangalore to call our own."

Richard opened his mouth to tell James the truth about Rajendra, how he had learned his own name in Mrs Hopkins' secret book, but there was a fierce light in James' eyes that gave him pause.

"It doesn't matter where we started from, or where we were born," James went on. "We can be heroes of *Britannia*. We can make them sit up and take notice of us because we are Miraculous and Extraordinary. Shield-brothers, like the knights of yore in that book you liked. The one with all the chivalry, and enchantresses, and swords and horses."

"Those knights all had Italian names."

"What does that matter? *We're* Britannian."

"You don't have a name?" Richard asked softly. "From your other life, before you came here? From Peking?"

"Liverpool," James admitted reluctantly. "I've never been to Peking. At least, not that I can remember. Honestly, I barely remember Liverpool. That's just the furthest back I know about."

Richard blinked. He shouldn't be surprised: if he felt any twinge of shock, it was that James had admitted it to him at all. "And the Romani?"

"That part's true, though mostly the travelling theatre troupe was around the Midlands, before we came south. They gave me plenty of names, but none of them stuck. I was the Extraordinary Rupert for a while, and the Amazing Absalom, and then they mostly called me Othello, after the black man in Shakespeare. I suppose Shakespeare never wrote a play about Chinamen. Have you read any Shakespeare?"

Richard shook his head slowly. *I have a name*, he wanted to say. But he knew nothing about Rajendra, nothing solid. Nothing that he knew to be real. And... James did not have a name.

"I want to be Rinaldo," he said finally. "You can be Orlando."

James grinned at him. No. *Orlando* grinned at him.

"We're brothers now," he said as the carriage drew them towards Buckingham Palace and a promised workshop of metal and magic to play with.

"Aren't we?"

"Of course," said Rinaldo. This, he could believe in. "We're brothers." The two of them, against the world. He needed nothing more.

END